IMMORTAL FOR THE PLOT

LOLA B. MARIE

Book Cover by Aurelia Dunbar of Mayonaka Designs

Edited by Jaquelyn Vale, She Who Edits, LLC.

For inquiries, please contact: **lola.b.marie.author@gmail.com**.

1st edition 2025

Contents

Also by Lola B. Marie

A Soul Seen

"I can't stay long...I see you, Emery. Come back to me."

It was supposed to be a one-time weekend at a haunted hotel—a wild, carefree bachelorette party for her sister. But for Emery, it became much more.

She kept coming back, drawn to him. From the moment their souls brushed against each other, Emery felt a connection that defied reason. Every encounter was a whirlwind of passion, leaving her questioning the line between dreams and reality. She was falling for a man who appeared only in her dreams...but who felt all too real.

Now Emery faces an impossible choice: remain rooted in reality without him, or seek him forever in her dreams.

A Soul Seen is a fast-paced, seductive novella about love that transcends reality, where Emery must discover if the passion she's found with Patrick is worth chasing—or if their love is destined to remain a fleeting, ethereal connection.

In My Boxes & Breakups Era

"I'm a different person than I was at 23 and as I peer ahead into my future – ten, twenty, thirty years down the road – tears fill my eyes at the prospect that *this* is the rest of my life. *I don't think I can accept that.*"

In a life marked by monotony and a marriage that has long since lost its spark, Jo finds herself yearning for something more—though she can't quite put a name to it. After taking a risk and opening her own clothing boutique, she begins to embrace her potential. She stands at the precipice of change, armed with newfound clarity about herself. She is no longer a bystander in her own life; she has the power to choose what aligns with her true self.

And through this journey of self-discovery and growth, there's Cole. The new UPS driver that delivers all her restocks, also brings his easy charm and soulful eyes to brighten up even the cloudiest of days.

Jo's journey has brought her to a crossroads, one full of challenges, but also brimming with possibilities. Her big decisions now hinge on her values and what kind of future she envisions. Does she attempt to rebuild her marriage, knowing the effort and compromise it would take? Or does she embrace the freedom that comes with walking away and the chance at a brighter future with someone new?

In My Boxes & Breakups Era is a contemporary romance about second chances in life, the search for self-worth, and the strength needed to grow.

To my one, true soulmate. To whom this book would not exist without. Kalie, you're the platonic love of my life. At the time this book comes out, we'll have been together almost 25 years. You've been here through every iteration of ME, and you're still here. Thank you. Also, to Christopher Moore—thank you for the inspiration.

Official Vibes Playlist

1. "Psycho Killer" – Talking Heads

2. "Rock Lobster" – The B-52s

3. "Modern Love" – David Bowie

4. "I Want Candy" – Bow Wow Wow

5. "Just Like Heaven" – The Cure

6. "Once in a Lifetime" – Talking Heads

7. "Private Idaho" – The B-52s

8. "Rebel Rebel" – David Bowie

9. "Love Plus One" – Haircut 100

10. "Tainted Love" – Soft Cell

11. "Ashes to Ashes" – David Bowie

12. "She Blinded Me with Science" – Thomas Dolby

13. "Whip It" – DEVO

14. "Let's Dance" – David Bowie

15. "Cruel to Be Kind" – Nick Lowe

16. "Bizarre Love Triangle" – New Order

17. "Planet Claire" – The B-52s

18. "In Between Days" – The Cure

19. "This Must Be the Place (Naive Melody)" – Talking Heads

20. "Under Pressure" – Queen & David Bowie

21. "Tempted" – Squeeze

22. "Is She Really Going Out with Him?" – Joe Jackson

23. "Echo Beach" – Martha and the Muffins

24. "Goodbye Horses" – Q Lazzarus

Note from the Author

CONTENT WARNINGS

SPOILER WARNING: Read on at your own risk. This will spoil one scene in the book that I personally believe is better when read without prior knowledge. However, your mental health matters. Please choose wisely.

.

.

.

Listen, our FMC is very obtuse and rarely considers the outcomes of her actions. But not in a malicious way! She goes into everything with the best of intentions. That being said, there is one scene that would be considered non-consensual. It's not a long scene, and the MMC puts an end to things very quickly. There is no violence, and no one leaves this encounter traumatized. (Though, Rose might be a little embarrassed.)

PROLOGUE

1825

My head swims as I sit on the edge of the bed, attempting to pull my pants up my legs. I blink a few times, hoping to clear the fog seeping in at the edges of my vision. After another moment, I stand, pulling my trousers up to my hips in one swift motion. The room spins violently, and suddenly the floor is coming up to meet me. Pain shoots through my head as my skull bounces against the hardwood. Black dots dance across my vision.

I lay still, trying to hold onto consciousness. I hear a muffled hiss, and the swishing of a skirt as Anne rushes into the room. Her clothes are still askew from the passionate moment we just shared, and she's carrying a small bucket. Too small to be the water bucket. A drop of red liquid drips down the side. *What is in that?*

My eyes start to roll back in my head, but I force my eyelids open, meeting Anne's gaze. Kneeling at my side, she brushes the hair from my forehead.

"Oh, Anthony. You were overcome so quickly." She tuts as she assesses my body, which, I realize, has begun to twitch. "I thought I had more time."

Her words make no sense to me. "Anne." My voice is barely there. "What...what's happening?"

"Shhhh," she croons. "It'll be over shortly."

Her cryptic words echo as I finally lose my grip on reality. All goes black.

CHAPTER ONE

DECISION MADE

Rose

Present Day

Pro: You stop gaining weight. Con: You stop losing weight.

Pro: No more food cravings. Con: No more yummy snacks.

Pro: Unlimited reading time. Con: ...no con for that.

As of now, all signs point to immortality being a pro. Alrighty then. Decision made.

All I want out of life is time. Time to read the ever-growing list of romantasy books on my TBR. Time to dive into every new series that intrigues me. Time to adventure with every badass FMC that starts out as a socially awkward recluse, like me. And, fortunately, this kind of time is an option for me. Kind of.

My computer pings, pulling me away from the pro/con list I have written in my notebook. An email hits my inbox showing a name and date. Another dead person, another dollar. I drag the email to my research folder before sighing and closing my notebook. Now is not the time to ponder my questionable decision.

Pulling on my headphones, I open Spotify and press play on my work playlist, which consists of Talking Heads, David Bowie, The B-52's—you know, good music. My browser is already open with multiple tabs that aid in my research as a freelance obituary writer. And for the next few hours, my mind is occupied with the task of taking a person's entire life and summing it up in a few short paragraphs.

I like to think there's an art to writing obituaries. The surviving family members want to show the best version of their dead loved one. But they also want to ensure they themselves are reflected in that life lived. Surviving adult children always want obituaries to show the parental side of their mother or father. Siblings want the childhood they shared with the person to shine through. Friends want people to see just who they've lost and why it's a tragedy. Obituaries are more reflective of the people remaining than the person who has died. And I walk that line all day, every day, catering to the selfish sides of grief.

I don't know if this is just overall cynicism or my blatant dislike of other humans. Which came first? Who knows. But it's progressively gotten worse as I've gotten older, and I've receded further and further into myself over the years. I mean, the man vs. bear debate should explain all you need to know about why I distance myself from other people. The world has gone fucking nuts, and I truly want no part of it.

This is why writing obituaries from the safety of my apartment and spending all my free time reading is the perfect life for me. But I'm about to be 40...okay, in eight years. But it's there! And lately I've had this weird, existential panic about all the amazing books and incredible stories I am going to miss out on. Which led me to my pro/con list.

I slide my notebook across the desk, flipping it open to my list. Scanning the lines, I realize my decision is still clear. I will become immortal. Next step is to formulate a plan to make that happen. The most important step of that plan being to find a vampire to bite me.

Since vampires are segregated from humans, this is going to be easier said than done. Our kinds have been separated for a century.

Once vampirism became public knowledge, laws were set in place to keep humans safe. One of those laws was the segregation of our kinds. There are also laws against human/vampire contact in any form, and vampires are swiftly prosecuted when those laws are broken. There are a few prisons around the world that have had alterations in order to hold vampires. And since vampires are beholden to the same laws humans are, as well as the "no touchy humans" law, it's not entirely uncommon to see news of a vampire being tried and convicted.

Humans rarely seek out vampires, as there's not a lot of incentive to be turned. Vampires don't have amazing powers. They have enhanced senses of smell along with natural night vision. And their stamina, speed, and strength *are* increased, but only relative to how you were as a human. So, if you became a vampire when you could bench press 100 pounds and run a 20-minute mile, you'd end up being able to bench press 200 pounds and run a 10-minute mile. While that does hold an advantage over some humans, you're not exactly peak apex predator.

This makes human/vampire interaction rare. And it's easy to enforce laws when the supernatural beings aren't really all that supernatural.

Our city is literally split down the middle; vampires on one side, humans on the other. The only access point that connects us is the blood donation center. All major cities are set up similarly, which is why you never see rural vampires. They're required to reside in a designated vampire territory so they can access the donated human blood.

Since vampires and humans have coexisted peacefully for over one hundred years, humans have been required to donate blood every other month. On the odd months, we have to be tested to ensure we remain free of any bloodborne diseases. Contrary to what popular culture tells us, vampires aren't really dead. It's more like their bodies are awake in a suspended animation state, which means they can still die. Severe injuries and bloodborne diseases are the only cause of death for vampires. Otherwise, they live forever. No one really knows what the initial cause of vampirism was or why seemingly healthy human bodies start requiring other human blood to live once they're turned. But extensive research continues throughout the world. Meanwhile, we continue donating blood and coexisting.

I check my calendar. My next blood donation is scheduled for next week. When I'm there, I'll just scope the place out and figure out how to get through to the other side. Perfect plan! How hard could this really be?

CHAPTER TWO

SURELY THIS WILL WORK

Rose

I get to the blood donation center about two hours before closing. I figure that gives me enough time to give blood and then find somewhere to hide. My plan is simple but foolproof. After they take my blood, I will ask to use the restroom before I leave. I will then hide in one of the stalls until the humans close our side of the center. Once all the humans leave, I will exit the bathroom and find where it connects to the vampires' side. Easy enough. Surely this will work.

The Queen of Shadows audiobook blares in my headphones as I swing open the door and step confidently into the center. Aelin would be proud of me. I decided what I wanted, and I made a plan to make it happen! If she can overthrow an entire evil species that has corrupted the people in her world, I can sneak into a blood bank.

I check in at the front desk before settling into one of the comfortable recliners reserved for donors. I lean my head back on the headrest and allow myself to sink into the story playing in my ears. I don't have to wait long until a phlebotomist is prepping my arm and inserting the collection needle. I keep my eyes closed, focusing on Aelin's reunion with Rowan, my favorite part of this particular book. Seriously, real life cannot be better than this. So, why spend time living in the real world when I could disappear into these worlds?

An hour later, I've been taped up and instructed to come back in a month for testing. I schedule my return appointment with the woman at the front desk before thanking her and asking where the restrooms are. Unable to withhold a sly smile, I head off in the direction she points. I turn off my audiobook, letting my headphones rest on my shoulders. I need to be focused and fully aware of my surroundings in order to accomplish the next part of my plan.

I head to the last stall in the bathroom. Stepping inside, I push the door closed, but not all the way. If someone comes to make sure the bathroom is clear before closing, I don't want to give them any reason to look closely. Then I turn to the toilet, pulling sanitary wipes out of my backpack purse. I wipe down the entire toilet seat before tossing the wipes in the sanitary napkin trash can attached to the wall. Turning to face the door, I step backwards, with a foot on each side of the toilet. Using my arms to brace myself on either side of the stall, I carefully step up onto the toilet seat, with a foot on each side of the seat. I squat down so my head isn't visible over the top of the stall.

Keeping my arms braced on the walls, I turn my wrist slightly to check the time on my watch. Twenty minutes until the center closes. Hopefully it doesn't take long to close this place up. Taking a deep breath, I settle in to wait.

***

Jesus Christ, I am out of shape. My legs are burning, my ass screaming from squatting in this position for so long. Surely, it's almost time to get out of here. I check my watch. *Oh, fuck off.* It's only been ten minutes.

***

This is the worst form of torture. I don't know how much longer I can hold out in this position. I clearly did not think this through.

The center just closed, but I have no way of knowing when it's cleared of people, so I'm stuck here for a little bit.

Aelin would be so disappointed in me. My legs are Jell-O and on the verge of completely giving out on me. I don't know how I'm going to walk when I get out of here.

The bathroom door suddenly creaks as someone pushes inside. I hear another stall door close before the door opens again, ushering another person inside. My heart is rapidly pounding within my chest from both the exertion of holding myself over this toilet, and the anxiety of possibly being caught in the next few seconds.

"Blair, you all done with your stuff? Ready to go?" The second person who walked in sounds like they're still standing near the door, but the way voices echo in tile bathrooms, I can't be sure.

The toilet in the far stall flushes, and I hear someone exit. "Yep, just have to wash my hands, and then we can go," Blair, I presume, answers.

"Alright, I'm going to grab my purse and meet you at the front door." The unnamed person opens the creaky bathroom door, and her footsteps fade.

A few seconds later, the water turns off, and I hear the rustling of paper towels before Blair exits the bathroom, flipping the light switch as she leaves, plunging me into darkness.

***

As quietly and carefully as I can manage, I step off the toilet, wincing as my legs protest the new movement. Once I am firmly planted on the floor, I start massaging some feeling back into my ass and upper thighs. Stepping out of my stall into the pitch-black bathroom, I stop and attempt some stretches that don't require me to get on the bathroom floor. Clearly, this floor is not cleaned often, seeing as no one bothered to do it as part of the closing procedures. This is a medical facility, for crying out loud.

I spend about ten minutes stretching, allowing what I hope is enough time for Blair and her coworker to get in their cars and leave. Then I shuffle in the dark until I reach the bathroom door and quietly slip out into the hallway. It's dark, but the emergency lights allow me to see without having to pull out my phone for the flashlight.

I meander my way down the hallway, opening doors and peeking inside. There are multiple offices, a breakroom, and a few private patient rooms before I open a door to a large lab. Well, lab is being generous. It's more of a super sterile storage room. Wire shelves line the walls, holding different colored totes with all the supplies necessary to draw hundreds of pints of human blood each day.

From what I understand, all blood donation centers are set up the same. There is only one access point that connects the human side to the vampire side, and it's through a large, walk-in refrigerator. Once the blood is donated, it is stored in the refrigerator. Then, once the humans close their side, the vampires come in and do whatever they do with the blood. So, I just need to find this fridge.

I figure I'll go through the fridge, and once I get to the vampire side, I'll ask whoever I find to bite me. Then I'll go about my life as an immortal. Easy peasy!

Scanning the lab slash storage room, I spot a large metal door with a pull handle on the front. A smile spreads over my face as I head towards the fridge. This is going so well! The pain in my legs is almost forgotten as I get closer to the fridge door, and thereby, closer to my goal of immortality.

I place my hand on the handle, close my eyes, take a deep breath, and then pull.

The door doesn't budge. I pull again. Still, the door stays closed. That's when I see the keyhole on the handle. It's locked. Why is it locked?

I can feel myself deflate. I made it so far. I was *this* close to fulfilling my dream! All to be thwarted by a locked fridge door.

Frustrated, I pull manically at the handle, despite knowing it's not going to open. I huff and puff, grunt and curse, as my frantic pulls on the handle switch to swift kicks to the door. This door wants to stop me? It's going to take my aggression!

Sweat beads my brow, and my breathing is labored, my legs once again crying in protest as I use them in a way they don't want to be used. And then suddenly, I'm being pushed back, my ass landing hard on the cold tile floor.

I huff a breath, and my eyes go wide as I see a pair of black sneakers attached to a pair of legs, wearing dark jeans, stepping out of the opening fridge door. My eyes travel up the jeans to a belted waist, up a dark green Henley, partially covered by a white lab coat, before meeting bright green eyes under a mop of curly brown hair.

He's beautiful. But clearly a vampire. The iris of his eyes take up the majority, leaving almost no whites. His pupils are slit like a cat, leaving me with an unsettled feeling, like I'm seeing something not quite right. Dark circles, almost bruises, line the bottom of each eye. But they don't take away from how strikingly handsome he is. His features are chiseled, his jawline sharp. He wears black glasses, which he adjusts on his nose before sliding a hand through his disheveled hair.

"What in the world are you doing?" His voice is low, quiet, and British! But his frustration is evident.

My brain forgets how to function, and I hear myself blurt, "OMG, you look like a grown-up Dave Rygalski!"

I do an internal facepalm as I watch his brows furrow before he takes a labored sigh and replies, "First of all, you're speaking, not texting. Just say 'Oh my God.'" He takes his glasses off to rub a palm over his eyes before continuing. "And second of all, who is Dave Rygalski?" He slides his glasses back on, meeting my gaze. "You know what, never mind. You need to leave."

He starts to turn back toward the fridge door, and I realize I can't let this opportunity slip through my fingers.

"Wait!" I holler at him as I pull myself up to standing. I refrain from lunging at him in an attempt to keep him in this room with me.

He turns, just slightly, letting me know I have his attention.

"I need your help," I say, tentatively.

His body angles toward me, his eyes meeting mine. His brows twitch, letting me know he's awaiting my pitch.

I inhale a large breath before blurting out, "I need you to bite me so I can be immortal."

His entire body freezes, visibly locking into place where he stands. His voice is a growly whisper when he says, "Is this a joke?"

"No, I'm serious. Please." I do my best attempt at sincere puppy-dog eyes.

"Absolutely not." He clears his throat before turning on his heel and slamming the fridge door behind him. I hear the lock click, as it seems to echo with my failure through the now quiet room.

Well, that did not go according to my plan. Time to go back to the drawing board.

Chapter Three

TRY, TRY AGAIN

Rose

One month later, Bryce Quinlan and friends are my accompanying soundtrack as I enter the blood donation center for my bimonthly testing. The half-human/half-fae woman is my inspiration for this attempt at immortality. Bryce's plans often went awry, but she never gave up. If at first you don't succeed, try, try again.

I've had an entire month to workshop my plan, and this time, it's going to work. Instead of hiding in the bathroom, I just need to sneak into the fridge before it's locked at the end of the day. Then I can waltz right through to the vampire side. Piece of cake.

After checking in at the front desk, I find a seat that allows me to angle my body so I can see down the hallway where the lab slash storage room is located. It's not a heavy traffic area, but people are popping in there every once in a while to grab additional supplies. I'm going to have to be as inconspicuous as possible, but I need to get in there quickly. Swift and sneaky. I got this.

"Rose?" My name is called, and my head swivels to the woman standing there. I smile brightly as I stand and make my way toward her. As I approach, I notice her nametag. Blair. I stifle my giggle. This woman has no idea that I was hiding in a bathroom stall while she relieved herself just a month ago.

Blair is quick and efficient, leaving me with about forty minutes until the center closes. I brought my hoodie, which is currently tied around my waist, but I can't sit in a refrigerator for forty minutes. I learned my lesson with the squatting. My body cannot handle much discomfort. So, I make my way to the bathroom to kill some time.

I close myself in a stall, turn my headphones on, and start doom-scrolling TikTok.

***

After taking a screenshot of yet another book recommendation video, I glance at my watch. *Fuck!* I only have ten minutes. Jesus, TikTok really does suck you in. Damn those algorithms.

I exit the stall, wash my hands quickly, and peek my head out of the bathroom. The hallway is currently clear, but I hear voices near the front desk. I need to be fast.

I scurry down the hallway, eyes darting each direction as I near the door to the storage room. Quietly, I open the door, peering into the room. *Whew.* It's empty. I duck inside, pulling my hoodie from around my waist as I close the door. I pull it on over my head, momentarily getting stuck on the headphones around my neck. Approaching the fridge door, I take a deep breath and place a tentative hand on the handle and pull.

It opens.

A smile immediately takes over my face. *I did it!*

I slide inside, and the lights automatically flicker on. The fridge is very large and is organized by blood type. I spot a corner that I can slip into that would keep me hidden if someone from the human side were to come in here within the next few minutes. I wedge myself into the corner, squatting down to make myself as small as possible. My legs protest just slightly. It took forever for the soreness to go away after my last attempt at this. One might have taken that as a sign to get in better shape. One is not me.

After a moment of stillness, the lights flicker off, plunging me into darkness. I bury my nose in the neckline of my hoodie to keep it warm. I keep my ears peeled for the lock of the human side to click. Once I hear that, I know I am good to go.

Time ticks by slowly as I wait for the sound of that lock, and my mind drifts to the vampire I saw here last month. I would be lying if I said this is the first time I've thought about him since our encounter. Those green eyes have starred in a few of my dreams since then. But in my dreams, he's less grumpy, more...accommodating, if you will. I giggle internally at the dirty direction my thoughts tend to go when those green eyes appear in my mind. While I truly would be intrigued to see him again, I kind of hope I don't. He did not seem keen on helping me meet my goal, so I hope I find a more willing vampire this time around.

All of a sudden, the lights flicker on, alerting me to movement in the fridge. I never heard the click of the lock, and my body tenses, waiting to see what's going to happen next. *That's what I get for daydreaming about a hot vampire, I guess.* Time seems to freeze as I wait for something, anything. And then I hear a deep sigh and the accented words that follow.

"Again? Really?" His voice is deep and gravelly from disuse. His British accent flows like water over the words, making them smooth and enticing, despite the obvious annoyance.

I peek my head out of the corner, immediately meeting his green-eyed gaze.

His eyes close as his chin drops to his chest. His hand travels up to pinch the bridge of his nose. I allow him this moment of irritation and fully step out of the corner before I speak.

"Funny meeting you here," I jest. His head snaps up again, his eyes glaring.

"What are you doing?"

I stand my ground. "I'm still on that mission to achieve immortality. Any chance you've changed your mind on helping with that?"

"No," he growls.

"Any chance you have a friend who is willing?" I smile politely as I wait for his response.

None comes.

My smile falters. "Do you...do you have a friend...like, at all?"

He glowers. "No one here will assist you with your asinine goal. I don't know what you're trying to do here, but you need to leave."

I decide to lean into my playful side. "Dodging the question doesn't bode well for you, sir. I'm starting to believe you're friendless." My lips quirk in a playful smile as I cross my arms across my chest, popping my hip out just a little.

"The state of my friendships are none of your concern." He starts walking toward me to usher me out the door. "You need to leave."

I lock my knees, attempting to stay firmly planted. "Wait, how did you know it was me?"

A pause, brief but noticeable. "You have a distinct smell." He doesn't make eye contact with me as he attempts to nudge me towards the door.

"A distinct smell? Like, in a good way or a bad way?"

His eyes finally meet mine. "Not in a bad way."

"Ooooh, what do I smell like?"

"It doesn't matter. Now come on, let's go."

"Please, please tell me! Now that you've brought it up, I really can't leave until I know."

He lets loose one of his deep sighs again. "Fresh rain in a field of wildflowers."

My breath catches in my chest. "Wow, that was oddly specific."

He blinks at me a few times, seeming flustered, before nudging my elbow again. "I answered your question. Now go."

"Why are you so grumpy? We could be friends? If you turned me into a vampire, I could be your new friend!" The fact that I am volunteering to befriend someone is completely uncharacteristic. I don't enjoy social situations, and the words spewing forth from my mouth right now seem to be coming from someone else. But I'm going to chalk it up to a means to an end. The ends justify the means. Whatever expression fits here.

"I don't need a friend. I just need you to leave." He stops abruptly. "You do realize that this isn't safe for you, correct?"

I balk. "What do you mean?"

Another deep sigh. "You're attempting to sneak into vampire territory, which is illegal because it's potentially dangerous to humans. You're a walking blood bag."

Ew. "I really did not need that visual."

"I really don't need you in my lab." He has successfully scooted me to the door leading to the human side of the blood center. I turn quickly, so my chest is almost flush with his. My skin warms at the closeness of our bodies.

"But *you* haven't attacked me or treated me like a walking blood bag?" He seems like a normal person other than the weirdly beautiful eyes and the deep circles under them.

A muscle in his jaw feathers as he takes a small step backwards before he answers. "I have more self-control than the average American vampire."

Intrigue! "Really, why? And why did you specify American? Do Americans overall have less self-control? I mean, that tracks..."

"Your questions are incessant."

"You know I'm not going to give up, right? I've made up my mind, and I'm going to figure this out. You'll see me again, sir!" I poke his chest as he leans around me to unlock and push open the door.

"I truly hope not..." He trails off as if wanting to say my name.

"Rose."

He looks at me, and his eyes ask the question his mouth doesn't need to.

"My name is Rose. And I'll see you next month."

"No, you won't, Rose. Do not attempt this again."

"Whatever you say..." I trail off, hoping he'll gift me with his name as well.

A long moment passes before he mutters, "Anthony."

I offer him a little wave as I turn and head to the door of the storage room. Pulling open the door, I call over my shoulder. "See you in a month, Anthony!"

I don't need eyes in the back of my head to see his eyes roll.

CHAPTER FOUR

THIRD TIME'S A CHARM?

Anthony

It's been thirty days since I last saw Rose, and I find myself wondering if I will see her today. Part of me hopes she has given up on this ridiculous fantasy. But an even larger part of myself hopes to see her. And I can't even begin to understand why. She's obnoxious. Obtuse. And rather annoying. Yet, since I saw her in that storage room two months ago, I find my errant thoughts traveling to her often.

And then seeing her in the fridge last month was quite a surprise. But, a pleasant one. Why? What is it about this woman?

I shake my head as I reach inside my fridge for a bottle of coconut water before grabbing my keys and starting my walk to work.

***

The walk from my apartment to the blood donation center isn't unpleasant. I live in the warehouse district, so there's a lot of nondescript buildings that have been converted to living quarters. But it's quiet, and since I'm heading west, I get to see the tail end of each sunset.

Life has become a bit tedious and mundane over the last century. I've seen a lot happen in the world over my last 200 years, and while some of it was exciting, most days have just bled into the next. However, no matter how many sunsets I've witnessed, each one is different. My nightly walks, watching the colors change over the sky as the sun sinks past the horizon are my reminder that there is beauty in life. I just wish I had found more.

***

The center is quiet when I enter. It doesn't take many of us to run our end of things. And we're all pretty spread out, depending on what our job consists of. I'm the single Quality Control Analyst at this location, and I process the samples submitted for bloodborne disease testing. It's important work, as it ensures any human who has caught such a disease is notified that they are no longer able to give the typically required blood. Seeing as we can still catch these diseases, it's imperative my job is completed with no errors.

I slip into my lab, setting my keys and water on my desk, sliding my lab coat on before heading to the door of the fridge.

The moment I open the door, I'm hit with a wave of her rainy wildflower scent before her small body barrels toward me, attempting to slip through the small opening in the door. My arm wraps around her waist as I hoist her into the air, stepping into the fridge and closing the door behind me.

I set her down, and she's immediately crossing her arms over her chest, a pout crossing over her features.

"Were you just lying in wait for me to open the door?"

"To be fair, I wasn't sure it was going to be you," she huffs, then adds, "and, as they say, third time's a charm." She shrugs.

I barely refrain from rolling my eyes. "I'm the only QCA working."

"How the hell do I know that?" She throws her hands in the air to emphasize her point.

A deep sigh escapes my chest. "Rose," I pause, and her brows quirk, waiting for me to finish. "I feel the need to ask what you're doing, but I assume you're just going to give me the same answer, yes?"

"Anthony. I am determined to become immortal, and you are not going to stop me."

"Your determination means nothing if your plan continues to be terrible. Seriously, what's next? You plan to hit me over the head to get past me? And what happens when you actually get through to the other side?"

Her hands go to her hips, clearly agitated that I called out her poor planning skills. "Determination means everything, Anthony. If I am determined to succeed, I will, just like the heroines in my books."

Heroines in her books. Is this woman living in a fantasy?

"As far as what happens when I get to the other side, that's the easy part! I find a vampire willing to turn me, and that's that!"

Jesus Christ. That's that?! I pinch the bridge of my nose, trying to withhold my inherent sense to scold her. "Rose," her name exits my mouth in a deep growl. "If you made it to another vampire, it's entirely likely that you would not leave the situation alive. Do you realize that? Most vampires would drain you, and it wouldn't even be intentional."

Her face pales a little, and her hands slide off her hips, resting limply at her sides. But I keep going. "Not to mention, if you found a vampire with the self-restraint to help you accomplish your mission, do you have the necessary paperwork showing you've gotten permission from the VHAA to be turned?"

When she answers, her voice is small. "VHAA?"

Oh, for fuck's sake. "Rose, the Vampire Human Alliance Agency. You have to obtain permission to be turned; otherwise, the vampire who turns you could be legally prosecuted. It's against the law. Plus, you need to be removed from the blood registry. There's red tape to cut through before making a decision like this. Did you do *any* research before you enacted this wild plan?"

Her eyes fall to the ground before she whispers, "I have so many questions."

Why does this woman want this so badly? Does she not understand the monotony she would be signing herself up for? "Why do you want to be immortal, Rose? What do you think you're going to get out of this?"

Her gaze lifts to meet mine, and I see the resolve return to her eyes. "Do you know how many books exist in the world? How many stories there are to be read? And everyday more and more people are getting more and more ideas that they are ready to start writing into the next epic fantasy series. I want to read them all, Anthony. I want to disappear into each and every world, fall in love, have adventure, meet new characters. I want to experience heartbreak, learn magic, find new paths. I can't do that if my life is cut short after 80 years."

As she's speaking, her face transforms with a brilliant smile. Her eyes seem to glow with the pleasure she clearly derives from reading. But..."Rose, you can do all of those things in real life. Go out and live your own adventure, fall in love, find the magic that exists in nature. You can have your own grand, epic adventure." My heart twists at the thought of her falling in love with someone else, with someone else leading her on the adventures she so greatly seeks. I don't have time to question why that is.

Her face falls again, and I hate being the one to cause it. "I can't live a grand adventure."

"Why?"

I can almost watch the wall build before my eyes. She doesn't want to explain herself to me, and why should she? "I just can't, okay? So, let me do this. Please."

I start to reach for her hand but think better of it, instead running my hand through my hair. "Rose, I can't do that."

Her head bows, hair falling in front of her face. But a moment later, it lifts, shaking the hair from in front of her eyes, her chin jutting into the air. "You're not going to ruin this for me, Anthony. I am going to make this happen." She marches toward the door at the opposite end of the fridge. Opening it, she steps through but turns to face me before closing it. Her face is a mask of irritation and determination. "You *will* see me again." With that, she slams the door, and I can't help but smile.

***

All night, images of Rose dance in my mind as I work. Her steely resolve brings me a strange sense of joy, and I find myself hoping she will get everything she wants in life. But I also feel an indescribable ache at the idea that this strangely incredible woman doesn't feel like she can have real-life adventure and love. What is holding her back?

It seems I've caught her determination bug because a sense of need flows over me. If I see her again, I will figure her out. And I will convince her to live her life, no matter how short, to the fullest. I may be stuck finding my only happiness in each sunset, but she doesn't have to be.

CHAPTER FIVE

HERE WE GO AGAIN

Rose

I 'm standing in the middle of the walk-in refrigerator, hands behind my back, when he opens the door. His strange green eyes immediately meet mine as he pauses in the doorway. Under his breath, I hear him mutter, "Here we go again." The volume of his voice increases when he addresses me. "Someone really should speak to the people on your side about better security. How do you keep getting in here?"

I ignore his question, feeling triumphant as I stomp toward him, finally brandishing the sheet of paper I held behind my back. I flap it in his face a few times before he reaches up and snatches it from me. His eyes peruse the words on the page, and my smile grows as his brows draw closer and closer together.

When his eyes finally meet mine again, I can't hold it in anymore. "Ha! I did it, and now you have to help me!" I point directly at his face, waiting for him to succumb to my wishes.

***

After Anthony literally caught me last month trying to get through to VampireLand—you know, like Disneyland, because it's where all *my* dreams will come true—I realized I was lacking some information. And while the revelation that I would need to get permission to be turned had me feeling wholly unprepared, I pulled myself up by the metaphorical bootstraps and took to Google. I located the closest VHAA office in my city and called to make an appointment. I was transferred to multiple people over the course of the call, all of them seeming very confused about what I wanted, but I was finally able to get an appointment to speak to someone in person.

Upon arriving, I told the front desk I was there to see Sharon, and—after waiting for what seemed an incredibly long amount of time, considering I had an appointment—I was escorted to a small office and handed a clipboard with a form for me to fill out. The office was small, with no windows. The overhead lights had a bulb that was out, casting half the room in shadow. I sat in one of the chairs settled in front of the small, brown wood desk, which was almost entirely bare of any working essentials and seemed to be coated in a thick layer of dust.

As I put my final signature on the form, a stern-looking woman waltzed in, rounding the desk and plopping down in the seat behind it. When she dropped the file folder she was holding onto the surface of the desk, a small plume of dust permeated the air. With a huff, the woman—Sharon, I presume—batted the particles out of the air and started brushing the remaining dust off the desk and onto the floor. I watched all of this, slightly enraptured by what was playing out before me.

Sharon finally met my gaze, harshly glaring at me over the rim of her glasses. "Ms. Miller, can you explain, again, why you're here?"

Irritation flashed across my face. I had already explained this to multiple people. But I forced a smile and pressed on. "Please, call me Rose. And I'm here to obtain the necessary permission to allow me to become immortal." I folded my hands in my lap, keeping hold of my smile.

Sharon just stared at me.

My smile faltered, and after another moment of silence from her, I spoke again. "Listen, Sharon—may I call you Sharon?—I just want to find a nice vampire to turn me so I can live a long, quiet life reading every romantasy book that catches my fancy. Is that really too much to ask?"

Her blinking continued, but I was done talking. I had explained what I wanted. Now, she needed to tell me if this was possible or not. I gripped the clipboard in my lap and sat back in my chair, content to wait.

She finally seemed to pull herself together and looked at the contents of the folder on the desk. "In all my time working here, this office has never been used. No request like this has ever come in. It's always been a possibility, but no one ever thought it would happen."

My brow furrowed. "No one has ever asked for permission to seek out a vampire to turn them?"

"Not in this city."

"Wow...that is not what I would have guessed."

She scrutinized me over her glasses once more. "Ms. Miller—Rose—are you sure you want this for yourself? You don't need to be immortal to live the life you're describing."

Irritation, again. Why did everyone keep asking me if I was sure, like I hadn't thought this through? I was a grown woman! I could and would make my own decisions in life.

I steeled my spine, tipping my chin slightly higher in the air. "I'm sure. I've had a lot of time to think about this, and it's what I want."

Her gaze was unflinching. But after a moment, she pulled a stamp and ink pad out of the old desk and gestured for my clipboard. Her eyes quickly perused the form before she huffed a resigned sigh and stamped her approval over my form. As she handed it back to me, she asked, "How, pray tell, are you going to find a vampire to turn you?"

I winked at her as I slid the form out of the clipboard. "You let me worry about that."

Later that afternoon, after office staff had made copies of my approved form and had given me further instructions on how to remove myself from the blood registry if I succeeded at my goal, I skipped out of the building, counting down the days until I could shove that piece of paper in Anthony's face.

***

My finger is still pointed at Anthony, my face alit with triumph. But Anthony doesn't even blink. My self-assuredness wavers, and I drop my hand. "I did what you said I had to do. I got permission, and I have the instructions on how to get off the blood registry. I did it!" My breathing is accelerating in frustration.

"Rose, just because you obtained permission doesn't mean I have to agree to this nonsensical plan you have." His voice is soft, almost timid, so unlike what I've heard from him before.

I turn and start pacing the small open space in the fridge. "No, no, you said I needed to do this. I did it." I stop and turn to him. "Why won't you help me? Or send me to someone who will?"

"Because, Rose, this is not a decision you should be making. You should just enjoy the life you have." His eyes are almost pleading, and I don't know how to respond. This encounter with him is entirely different, and I'm a little off balance.

After a moment, he steps aside, gently grabbing my elbow and ushering me onto his side of the fridge. My heart leaps at the thought that he's changed his mind. We step out the door and into an actual lab setting. He guides me to a desk and gestures for me to sit before stepping back in the fridge and returning with a case of samples.

"I'm going to work. And while I work, I'll allow you to ask some questions. And hopefully, by the end of our time together tonight, you will see that immortality is not all it's cracked up to be. How does that sound?" He eyes me, questioningly. A strange sense of hope spears through my chest. I nod at him in response. "Good, let me get this started, and then we can talk."

With his back turned, I can't help but let a mischievous smile tilt my lips. He thinks he's going to change my mind, but now I am determined to change his. He's going to end up helping me, goddamn it.

***

"Who is Dave Rygalski?"

My involuntary laughter causes me to nearly choke on the drink of water I had just taken. Recovering, I answer with, "Really? You get twenty questions, and that's what you want to use one for?"

He shrugs. "You said I look like a grown version of him. I want to know who that is."

An hour has passed since we started this game of twenty questions. So far, I've been attempting to get information about Anthony himself, but his answers have been short and sweet, offering no real insight into who he is.

I spin in the office chair I've been camped in. "He's Lane's first—and best—boyfriend in Gilmore Girls. Played by Adam Brody, pre The O.C. days."

His eyes shoot to me over the table he's working at. "He's from a television show? I thought he was a real person." His voice is haughty as he rolls his eyes and mutters, "What a waste of a question."

I laugh. "I could have told you it was a waste." I wait for his eyes to meet mine again, and I shoot him a wink before spinning another rotation in my chair. On my way around, I grab the bottle of coconut water off the desk, taking another sip. Then it occurs to me. "Why do you have this in here? I thought the only sustenance a vampire needs is human blood?"

He pauses his work. "Did you know that coconut water was reportedly given intravenously to severely dehydrated soldiers in World War II?" I shake my head, and he continues, "With that report, other Western countries, including my own, did a study to see how coconut water could affect vampires. They found that a vampire could subsist on one pint of human blood per week if they supplement with coconut water. European countries decided it made more sense for vampires to live like this than to require so much human blood be donated."

"How much blood does a vampire need if they aren't drinking coconut water?"

"One pint every two days." He returns his focus to his work.

"Why doesn't America implement that lifestyle?" We already had a medical shortage of some blood types. If there was a way to require less human blood, why wouldn't we do it?

"Why doesn't America ban Red Dye 40? There are a lot of things that European countries have banned because of how bad they are for the human body, and yet America doesn't follow suit." He shrugs. "America is the country of excess, and no one wants to be told what they can and can't put in their bodies."

"And yet everyone wants to tell women what we can and can't do with our bodies," I huff. Anthony eyes me over his glasses. "Sorry, moving on. So, is your coconut water consumption the reason you have more control when you're around me?"

I watch him move fluidly around his space as he answers me. "Correct. I don't require as much human blood, so my drive for it has lessened. American vampires still feel the need for it since they are limited to a very specific amount and are getting nothing in between meals, so to say."

I realize there's a lot about vampirism that I don't actually know, so I decide to keep rolling with my information-seeking questions. "Why don't you have fangs? Do you actually have an aversion to sunlight? What's with the weird eyes?" I didn't mean to blurt it all out, and I dart my eyes to see Anthony's reaction.

He smirks before saying, "That fully counts as three questions."

I laugh. "Fair."

He continues processing samples as he answers. "Bones don't change when a body goes through the transition. And since teeth are bones, they stay the same. Human teeth are perfectly capable of ripping through muscle and sinew, so, evolutionarily, it wouldn't matter anyway. We can still hunt, if necessary."

I swallow at the idea of him hunting. But strangely, I can't tell if I'm scared or intrigued. Before I can question it further, he continues.

"We don't have an actual aversion to sunlight. The fact that most of us have pale skin is a byproduct of the laws enacted to keep our kinds apart. We mainly operate overnight, while humans still operate during the day." He looks up, a flirty smile crossing his lips. "I have an excuse to be melanin challenged. What's yours?"

I toss the cap of my water at him, but he catches it effortlessly. Walking over to me, he sets it on the desk next to me. Before he goes back to his station, he leans over me in the chair, bringing our faces incredibly close. My breath hitches, wondering what he's going to do next. Then a sly smile flashes over his face as he spins the chair and walks back to his table.

I can't help my laugh as my chair continues to spin, slowing, before coming to a stop facing him. He's watching me with a look on his face I can't quite decipher. But then he clears his throat and goes back to work. Wanting to move past this strange moment, I prompt the last question. "And the eyes?"

"Ah, the eyes do go through a change during the transition. Our irises expand, and our pupils change shape. This is how we end up with enhanced night vision. It's common for predators. The permanent bruising is a result of the ocular muscles shifting to accommodate this change."

"Enhanced sense of smell, better night vision. Any other cool benefits I should know about?" I tick off on my fingers as I speak.

His glance turns wary. "Rose, I am not trying to sell you on vampirism. There aren't real benefits to this other than the extended lifespan."

I shrug. "I don't need any cool powers. The prolonged life thing is enough for me."

His head falls in defeat, his palms pressing on the metal table. Another resigned sigh leaves his lips, and I know I'm no closer to convincing him to help me than I was when I started this whole thing.

Anthony checks the watch on his wrist before looking back at me. "We need to get you back."

My stomach drops at the thought of leaving. I've thoroughly enjoyed my time with him, and if I leave here, I have to figure out another plan to get back. I refuse to give up.

Anthony approaches my chair, stopping just a few feet in front of me, waiting for me to stand. I watch him closely for a moment, neither of us speaking. Finally, I internally concede. He won tonight. But I'm not done trying. I stand, leaving the water bottle on the desk and heading toward him. As I approach him, he shifts to walk side by side with me to the walk-in fridge, causing our hands to brush. I could swear a zap of energy passes from his skin to mine. And based on his sharp intake of breath, he felt it too.

I step into the fridge, turning to him before he closes the door. "Thank you for tonight, Anthony. You've given me a lot to think about, and I appreciate you answering my questions."

"You're welcome, Rose." A sadness shines in his eyes. "I hope to never see you again."

His words feel like a punch to the gut, and by the time I've recovered, he's closed the door.

CHAPTER SIX

GROUNDHOG DAY

Anthony

The closer I get to the thirty-day mark, the more anxious I feel. The moment I saw Rose's face fall when I told her I hope I never see her again, I wished I could take the words back. Rip them right out of the air and put that vibrant smile back on her face. But the idea of her throwing away what could be a beautiful future was enough to make me close the door and return to my work. The image of her standing there has plagued my thoughts since.

Now, we are in the window of time where she would be returning to give her required blood, and all I want to do is apologize. Tell her I'm sorry for breaking her spirit, even if for just a moment, and beg her to forgive me. But also, beg her to reconsider her choices. Each evening when I first open the fridge door, my senses heighten—a stress response from worrying she'll be standing there. And then my spirits fall when she's not. The conflicting emotions are truly exhausting.

A light rain falls as I exit my building, muting the vibrant colors I'm used to seeing. The setting sun hidden behind the gray rain clouds just brings back the image of Rose in that refrigerator. Her light was stifled by my storm. Small gusts of wind splatter me with rain, leaving me covered in half of her signature scent. All I'm missing are the wildflowers. I close my eyes, inhaling deeply through my nose, before venturing out.

***

Once again, I walk face-first into her scent, like walking into a brick wall. With each interaction, it just grows stronger. And it seems the stronger her scent gets, the slower my reflexes get, because the next moment, Rose is standing before me, a piercing anger shining in her eyes and a small blade in her hand, aimed at my throat. I stop, waiting to see what she does next.

"Now, you listen here, Anthony..." she trails off for a moment. "Goddamn it, I wish I knew your last name. It would make this moment a lot more dramatic." She reinforces her hold on the knife, the pressure of the tip against my skin increasing slightly. "You are going to help me make my dream come true, or so help me!"

I wait for the rest of the threat to come, but it never does. "So help you what, Rose? What are you going to do?"

Her brow furrows. "Don't test me, Anthony!"

It's difficult to withhold my amusement, but I keep my voice even when I respond. "Rose, what was your plan here? What happens next?"

"I can't keep living like it's Groundhog Day! Seriously, Anthony, I will get stabby!" Despite being so very serious, her eccentricities shine through, and my control of my facial features breaks, letting a smile slip.

The arm holding the knife drops, and her head bows in defeat. If my heart were beating, it would stop here and now. The smile I had accidentally shown her seconds before vanishes. Seeing her like this pains me greatly, and these feelings are puzzling. I reach for the hand holding the knife, slowly easing the weapon from her grip as she answers.

"You don't understand, Anthony. I need this, okay? Why do you care, anyway?" Her eyes plead with me to explain or change my mind, and I have the sudden urge to hold her and tell her how much her life is worth. How lucky she is to have a future that has the potential to change and morph as she continues to grow. But I don't give in to the urge; instead, I pocket the knife and gently wrap her hand in mine, leading her out of the fridge into my lab.

I lead her back to the seat she occupied last time, motioning for her to sit. Kneeling in front of her, I grab both of her hands as my eyes meet hers. "Rose, tell me why. Truly. Make me understand why an immortal life spent reading stories is a better alternative to a life well lived."

She glances away, offering me a self-deprecating chuckle. "You don't want to hear my villain origin story."

I graze her jaw with my thumb, guiding her eyes back to me before reclasping our hands. "You could never be a villain, Rose."

A sad smile passes her lips as she seems to contemplate me for a moment. She must find something worthy in me because she takes a deep breath and begins.

"When I was six, my parents and I got in a car accident. I made it out with minor injuries, but my parents weren't as lucky. My dad died on impact. My mom died in the hospital a day later."

Her eyes are on our entwined hands resting in her lap.

"I didn't have any other family, so I ended up in the foster care system. Relative to many other kids, I got out unscathed. I lived in the same household from age seven until I turned eighteen and could legally leave. I saw a few other kids come and go through the years, but I did what I could to be 'easy' so they'd keep me. My foster parents weren't abusive or neglectful. I always had food and clothes. The lights were always on, and I always had what I needed for school. But there was no love. Emotionally, they were absent."

She inhales a deep breath.

"I can't blame them, really. They did what they could to help give a safe space to kids who had lost everything. And, again, compared to a lot of other situations, they were amazing. But I was lonely and...empty."

Her eyes shift back to me, and I offer her a slight nod, urging her to continue.

"In fifth grade, we read Bridge to Terabithia, and it almost broke me. I couldn't understand why a story would be so sad. If it was fictional, why write pain? There was enough real pain in the world. My teacher took pity on me and started bringing me other books. Fantasy stories where the main character had to battle through the toughest of times but always found their peace and happiness at the end."

My frozen heart is breaking, hearing about young Rose. Imagining her, lost and alone, finding her only solace in literature, not other people. How she ended up this apparent ball of light and energy astounds me.

"Once I fell into these stories, I found all the things I was missing in my real life. And I never looked back. I've read hundreds, probably thousands, of books over the years. And with romance stories on the rise, discovering romantasy books was a wonderful surprise. I could have it all. I could have it all by reading these books."

Her eyes meet mine again, and staring out at me is the sad, scared, lost little girl. She never left. She still lives within Rose and is the driving force behind this entire endeavor. How can I show her that, if she just heals that little girl, she wouldn't be afraid to go out in the world and have real, wonderful experiences?

I stand quickly, an idea forming. Her head jerks up, following my movements. "What are you doing?"

I don't answer her, instead grabbing my phone and sending a text to the on-call QCA, asking him to come cover for me. He responds immediately, stating he will head this way. I pocket my phone and grab my keys off the desk.

I grab Rose's hand, urging her to stand. "Rose, I understand now, but I still think you are making a mistake. Give me tonight. Come with me and let me try to change your mind. If I don't, I'll find someone willing to turn you."

Her brow furrows. "Why couldn't you just do it?"

I swallow, unsure how to answer. Absently, I scratch the back of my neck, and if I could blush, I know my cheeks would be a deep pink. "I just can't, Rose. Okay?"

She looks at me for a long moment, and I internally beg her not to ask any follow-up questions. Finally, she nods.

"You'll come with me?" I ask her.

"Yes," she whispers.

Placing both hands on her shoulders, I urge her to pay close atten-tion. "Rose, when we leave this lab, you have to stay quiet and follow my every direction. Letting you past this point could be dangerous, so I need you to listen to me, okay?"

"Okay," she agrees.

"I'm serious, Rose. Keep that stubborn streak tucked away. Push down that urge to be stabby."

She rolls her eyes but smiles. "Okay!"

I hold her in my gaze for an extra beat before turning and heading for the door. With her hand in mine, we head out on Rose's first real adventure.

CHAPTER SEVEN

IT'S HAPPENING!

Rose

Right now, I feel like Michael Scott is living in my brain because all I hear is, "It's happening!" That scene from The Office is playing on a loop in my mind until Anthony gives me a pointed look, like he knows I'm not fully paying attention. But I'm elated at this turn of events. He might not know it yet, but this excursion is going to end in me being immortal.

I silence my internal soundtrack as he eases the door of the lab open. After looking down both sides of the hallway, he steps out, waving me after him. He quickly closes the lab and starts off down the hallway at a brisk pace. I hustle to catch up to him.

"We need to get out of here quickly. It'll be easier to be inconspicuous once we get outside," he whispers. I nod, even though he isn't looking at me, and follow where he leads. I don't bother paying attention to our surroundings as we head to the exit of the donation center. I don't plan on doing this again. Not alone, anyway.

But it's that moment that I wonder if I've been incredibly naïve. I'm putting blind trust in a man I've met a handful of times, and of those times, only one of them lasted longer than a few minutes. *Wait, man? This isn't even a man. This is a vampire.* One who has repeatedly told me that it would be dangerous for me to go out into VampireLand, and now he's willfully leading me there! The heroines in my books would *never!* But I'm in this now, so to make myself feel better about my reckless choices, I vow to be attentive and focused. I will not be caught off guard!

"Almost there."

Anthony's muttered words break the silence, cutting through my internal dialogue, startling me. A loud squeal comes out of my mouth before I can stop it. It doesn't even take him a second to respond. Anthony spins to face me, clutching the back of my head in one hand and wrapping the palm of his other hand over my mouth. My eyes go wide as I meet his furious green gaze, and a frisson of lust shoots through my body. His fingers curl just slightly in my hair as his fingers tighten their grip on my cheek. I have to fight to keep my eyes from rolling back in my head. Well, kink unlocked. Apparently, I like to be manhandled.

"Why do you struggle to follow simple directions?" His whisper is almost a growl. "Keep quiet, Rose."

I have to repress a moan at his demanding tone, but I manage a nod. Our eyes are locked, and I can see his pupils dilate. *Maybe he's as affected as I am. Wait, do vampires get aroused?* After another second, he releases me, grabbing my wrist and pulling me after him.

We reach a side exit with no further incident, and we step out into an empty alley. Anthony drops the hold he has on my wrist and runs his hands through his hair.

Turning to me, he asks, "Is it possible for you to go five minutes without drawing attention to yourself?"

I hope that's a rhetorical question, because I am not thinking clearly. My heart races, and my chest heaves. There's a low throb emanating from my core. I don't think I've ever experienced this level of attraction to someone. When he continues to stare at me, impatiently, I realize he's waiting for an answer.

"Yes?" I say, quietly.

"Yes? Is that a question? Are you implying you're not sure?" He huffs, clearly irritated with me.

"I will certainly try! I don't know what you want from me. This whole thing is crazy. I'm doing my best!"

He glowers at me, stepping into my space. He tilts his head down so our faces are inches apart. I can't help but swallow, and I watch his eyes dart to my throat to track the movement. "You agreed to this, Rose. If you can't handle it, I can get you back to the lab, through the fridge, and back to your life." He places his hand on the doorknob for emphasis.

"No, no, I can do this." I steel my spine, stepping back from him to take a gulp of fresh air. "I won't draw attention to myself. I'll be quiet."

With a sigh, he runs his hands through his hair again. "You're making me regret this," he mumbles. But then he grabs my hand again, pulling me to the mouth of the alley. "Stick to my side. We are going to keep to back alleys as much as possible."

With one hand held in his, I wrap my other hand around his bicep as we step out of the alley and begin our walk. To anyone who actually catches a glimpse of us, we're just a happy couple out for a stroll.

Wait—"Where are we going?"

He looks down at me with a small smile. "You really should have asked that before we even left, you know?" He chuckles. "It's as if you lack all sense of self-preservation."

He's not entirely wrong. "Well, are you going to tell me?"

"I'm taking you back to my apartment. On the way, you'll get a glimpse of our side, and maybe you'll realize it's not all that exciting."

"It's not about excitement for me, Anthony. This could be the most boring place in the world, and I'd still want immortality. In fact, boring is great, considering all I want to do is sit peacefully and read."

His grip on my hand tightens for a moment, his eyes boring into mine. "But you could do more, Rose. You could live an entire life."

The way he says that, it's as if he's lost an entire life. And I realize that I know nothing about him or how he got to be here. He sees my frown, mistaking my train of thought.

"I know, I'm a broken record. But I have to try to convince you." He gives me a little wink that should not be as sexy as it is.

We walk in silence for a few moments, my thoughts swirling between the heated attraction I feel towards him and my desire to know him. Again, he breaks the silence, but this time, I don't overreact.

"Bishop."

Confused, I utter, "What?"

"You said you wished you knew my last name. It's Bishop."

I smile up at him. "So, what's your story, Bishop?"

He pats the hand that's holding his bicep. "All in good time, Rose. All in good time."

CHAPTER EIGHT

THE PERFECT BLONDE ALE

Gavin

That smell.

What is that smell?

It's utterly perfect. Heavy notes of floral bring out the perfectly subtle sweetness, combined with petrichor to add a hint of bitterness.

I look around, trying to pinpoint where that incredible scent is coming from.

There's not much around that could elicit this enticing aroma. I'm in the warehouse district, for crying out loud.

But then I spot her.

She's holding the arm of a male vampire, but she's distinctly human. Her eyes give her away as they dart around, taking in her surroundings. Her neck cranes as her blatant curiosity encourages her not to miss a thing. The couple just passed me, and I hadn't paid them a second glance until her fragrance hit my nostrils. *What is she doing on this side of the city?*

I make the split-second decision to follow them, turning back the way I came, my previous destination forgotten. I keep a healthy distance between us, so as not to arouse suspicion. The rain has stopped, but the winds from the passing storm are still gusting, bringing her delicious perfume to me on the back of each breeze.

This woman was sent to me. And I am determined to make her mine.

She'd make the perfect blonde ale.

CHAPTER NINE

TELL ME YOUR STORY?

Anthony

Rarely do I ever enter into anything without a decent plan. Tonight, I did just that. Leading Rose out of the donation center, I was struggling to come up with a worthy adventure that would also keep her safe on this side of town. But then her comment about not wanting adventure rendered that idea moot regardless.

My only hope at this point is to offer her some connection. Show her that getting out there, taking risks, being vulnerable, could lead to something beautiful, if she only gave it a chance.

That's how I found myself ushering her through my side of the city, constantly hissing at her to keep her head down. Her blonde hair shone in the moonlight, already making us noticeable. But her sightseeing tendencies and not-so-quietly asked questions made it worse. So, when I finally guide her into the freight elevator that leads to my apartment, I let out a soft sigh of relief.

"This is a giant elevator!"

I resist an eye roll, trying to keep my agitation from bleeding onto her. "Yes, well, this is a converted warehouse."

"It's so cool!" Her eyes meet mine, and I'm momentarily stunned by the glint of excitement shining in hers. Maybe my plan will work after all.

The elevator pings as it stops at my unit, and I slide the large door open. My hand lands on her lower back as we step out and a feeling of familiarity rushes through me. Like my hand is meant to touch her, to guide her. I hastily break the contact, rushing to hang my keys on the hook by the door.

Turning back to Rose, I watch her eyes roam over my space, and I wonder how it looks from her perspective. It's a large, open concept, with the kitchen and dining area to the right, living room to the left. Large wall-to-wall windows line the living room and carry into the bedroom that was constructed in the back left corner. The bedroom has an en suite bathroom that also has a door to access it from the main room.

My living room is not set up as is typical, especially for Americans. A large, deep green area rug covers most of the space, on top of which sit two large armchairs, set side-by-side with an end table in between them. A low coffee table is centered in front. The sliding door off the elevator opens towards the kitchen, leaving the rest of the wall in the living room lined with bookshelves. The interior walls are painted a deep burgundy, with the exception of the kitchen, which is painted a warm gray. Navy cabinets offset the lighter color of the kitchen walls, pairing with my cream-colored tufted upholstered dining chairs, set around a long, driftwood dining table. Abstract art is placed strategically throughout the apartment, hanging on the limited amount of open wall space.

My eyes shoot back to her after my quick perusal, and I realize I'm holding my breath, hoping she finds it to her liking.

"Wow..." she trails off.

I clear my throat, awaiting the rest of her thoughts.

"This is beautiful. I wouldn't have pictured something so...warm." She turns to me and offers me a small smile.

"What, you pictured something cold and clinical?" I give her a teasing smirk, and I'm rewarded with a tiny giggle.

"I mean, kind of. But this is not that." She walks around, taking in the art hanging on the walls before heading over to the bookshelves. "You have so many books," she breathes.

I make my way to her, standing just next to her as she stretches on her tiptoes to see the top shelves then ducks down to see the bottoms. "This is how I like to spend my free time." I inwardly cringe at the similarity my life has to the one she wants. Maybe this wasn't such a good place to bring her.

She straightens and turns to face the two armchairs. "No couch? No TV?" she asks, plopping herself into one of the chairs.

I stiffen at the sight of her so comfortable in my home. And once again, I question why I brought her here.

She lifts her brows, still waiting for me to answer her question. "Um, no." I run my hand through my hair—a nervous habit. "I rarely have anyone over, so there's no use for a couch. And I don't really watch television. I have a laptop that I can watch movies on, if I feel in the mood."

I clear my throat, suddenly keenly aware of her eyes on me, and I rush to the kitchen to pull two bottles of coconut water out of the fridge. I turn to see that she has followed me, and I hand her one of the bottles, our fingers brushing as she takes it from me. Her breath hitches, and I see her cheeks warm with a blush.

"So, what now?" she asks, cracking open the seal on the bottle and taking a small sip.

"Now," I lean towards her with intention, "I make my pitch and hope you choose life."

***

All residents in my building have rooftop access, but I've never encountered anyone up here. Slowly, over the years, I've built a little haven for myself. A large pergola, draped in outdoor fairy lights, covers the small seating area I've arranged. A black, rattan patio sectional set faces a gas-powered, outdoor fireplace. Flower boxes line one section of the rooftop railing.

Again, I find myself waiting with bated breath to see how Rose reacts.

"Did you do this?" she whispers.

"I did." I pause as she continues to peer around, in awe of the beautiful space. "I enjoy being outside, in nature. But my options are limited in this territory."

She turns to me, a sadness dulling her eyes. "I'm sorry."

I wave her over to the sectional sofa. "Not to worry. I made my own natural space here."

She sits down, pulling her legs up and under her. "Does anyone bother it?"

"I've never seen anyone up here. And I've never seen any sign that someone else uses it." I shrug. "So, if they do, they're respectful, and that's all that matters."

"You continue to surprise me, Anthony."

"Yes, well, my accent tends to lead people to incorrect assumptions, I'm afraid." I take a sip of my coconut water.

"Are you going to set me straight?" Her smile is teasing. "Tell me your story?"

A resigned sigh escapes my lips. "I suppose I should."

The night is a bit chilly after the storms, so I stand to turn on the fireplace before settling back to tell her where I came from.

"I was born into a well-to-do family in London in 1795. I had excellent primary and secondary schools, which eventually helped foster my intense interest in the sciences. Back then, there wasn't as much information, but the strides we were making fascinated me, specifically as it pertained to biology and medicine. Jobs in the sciences were much more limited back then as well, so, when it came time to choose a university, I left London and journeyed to France. I studied at the University of Auvergne, now known as Université d'Auvergne Clermont-Ferrand. When I graduated, I returned to London, having secured a position at St. Bartholomew's Hospital."

I paused to take a sip of my coconut water, peeking at Rose over the lip of my bottle. She had leaned toward me, the captivated look in her eyes letting me know I wasn't boring her.

"Once I returned to London, I was working long hours but loving every minute of it. In my free time, I was doing additional study and following the likes of Christian Friedrich Nasse. I was twenty-five when Nasse's law was formulated, stating that hemophilia only occurs in males but is transmitted through asymptomatic females. I was completely fascinated and wanted to soak up all the information I could. My mother kept pestering me about getting married and settling down. But I felt I was in the prime of my life! I should take advantage of the time while I had the energy to continue learning.

It's not that I didn't want to get married. I knew I wanted to start a family; find a woman I enjoyed being with and have children of my own. I was looking forward to that chapter in my life, but I didn't want to cut the current chapter short for it. I thought I had plenty of time."

My breath catches in my chest as I think about the next part of my story. I look down at my lap, allowing myself a moment. A warm touch to my forearm startles me, and I turn to see Rose has slid closer to me on the sofa. Her hand tentatively grazes my forearm, offering silent comfort. A sad smile passes over my lips before I continue.

"Working late shifts at the hospital, I came to know a woman named Anne. She volunteered from time to time, but her appearances were never consistent. I found her a little odd, but charming. And beautiful. And after talking to her a few times, I found that she was just as inquisitive as I was. Conversation with her was easy. We discussed new discoveries in medicine and what other scientists' work we revered. I was completely taken with this incredibly intelligent woman. So, when she asked me to walk her home after a particularly grueling shift, I readily agreed. We talked the entire way, never falling into stunted silences. When we reached her door, she asked if I'd like to come inside. I was taken aback by her forwardness and the scandalous nature of her request. But I was also intrigued and very attracted to her. I couldn't bring myself to turn her down.

We shared a drink before she led me to her bedroom. It was like no sexual experience I had had before. She took charge, leading the entire way. It's all a blur now, but almost immediately after, I felt incredibly unwell before passing out entirely. When I awoke, Anne was feeding me blood from a ladle in a bucket. I found out later she would take blood from patients suffering minor injuries in the hospital. It ended up being what ultimately killed her when she drank blood from a patient with cholera. We didn't know at the time that bloodborne diseases could impact us. The cholera kept her from keeping down any blood she drank, leading to dehydration and malnutrition."

I stopped, inhaling a deep breath. Rose's hand still rested on my forearm, her nails tracing idle circles over my shirt sleeve.

"After I woke up with Anne, she explained with utter excitement that she was experimenting with me. She thought she knew how to replicate what she was and wanted to try it with someone she thought would appreciate it. She was thrilled to tell me about vampirism and all that was known about us at that time, thinking I would be happy to be a part of this new 'species.' But I was devastated. I knew that the life I had planned was no longer an option. And she took it from me against my will. I turned furious, leaving her and never looking back. I went into hiding for many years, knowing my kind would not be allowed to live. Anytime a vampire was discovered back then, they were beheaded. We were called demons, sent by the devil himself. I had to abandon my parents. They never knew what happened to me. I left everything behind to hide away and hope that time would bring advancements.

And it did, but it took a good long while. Once we could mainstream into society, I got a job and went back to school. Getting to learn all the amazing new advancements made by the scientific community was thrilling. And while my life had purpose again, I still feel the loss of potential every day. And I can't help but dwell on what I'll never have because of the choice of one selfish woman. I came to America to change my scenery, get away from the locations in my past that held me in my misery. It's been easier since I've been here, but I still wouldn't wish this existence on anyone."

I realize I had been staring at her hand through all this and finally dragged my gaze up to hers. Unshed tears filled her eyes, her sympathy for me shining brightly.

"I'm sorry that happened to you, Anthony. I'm sorry your life was taken from you."

She sits up on her knees, leaning into me, and before I realize what she's doing, she's pulled me into a hug. Her arms wrap around me, pulling me tightly to her, and after a moment, I wrap my arms around her in return. My head ducks down, burying in the crook of her neck. My lips hover over her skin, my breath washing over her as I whisper, "Thank you."

We sit like that for a long while, as I soak up the comfort of another person, something I haven't felt in many years. And then the irony hits me; I brought her here to offer her connection, but instead, she offered it to me.

When we finally break apart, she stares at her lap for a moment before quietly whispering the last words I want to hear. "Your story is truly heartbreaking, Anthony. And if I could change it for you, I would. But this life that was thrust upon you would be one I willingly choose for myself. I know what I'm giving up, but I also know what I'm getting in return. This doesn't change my mind."

My failure manifests in a dull throb at the base of my skull. I pinch the bridge of my nose, closing my eyes. When I open them, I glance past Rose to the skyline behind her, realizing the sun has started to rise. The human side of the blood donation center will open soon, filling with diligent workers and patients; it's too late to get her back through unnoticed today.

I stand up, grabbing her hand and pulling her up with me. "You're going to have to stay here until the sun sets. Then I'll take you back to the blood donation center so you can go home."

She grabs my arm, panic lacing her features. "But you said you'd find someone to help me."

I sigh. "And I will, Rose. But it'll take me more than a few hours. We'll get you back home where it's safe, and I'll let you know when I find someone."

"How will you let me know?" she asks.

"We can exchange phone numbers before you go home tomorrow. For now, can we get some rest?"

She nods before letting me lead her through the rooftop door and back down to my apartment.

Chapter Ten

IT'S MY FAVORITE TROPE!

Rose

Anthony's story replayed in my mind as he led me back down the stairs and into his apartment. My heart had broken for him as we sat on that rooftop. The life he had envisioned was taken from him, and he was determined to make sure mine wasn't. But I didn't have the same vision for my future. I didn't see a loving partner and children. The idea of having people that rely on me sends anxiety coursing through me. I never learned how to make true connections with people. There was no way I *wouldn't* disappoint someone who chose to put their trust in me. When times got hard, I fled into my books. Textbook dissociation, I know. But it worked for me.

The sound of a door latching shakes me from the thought spiral I had been lost to, and I realize we've made it back inside Anthony's apartment. Anthony's *gorgeous* apartment. I can't help but admire it all over again. I want to live here. I want to bathe in the warmth he's created in this space. *Warmth.* His arms around me in that long hug on the rooftop were warm. I never wanted him to let me go. And suddenly my pulse is racing from thoughts of a simple hug. *But was it simple?*

"I know it'll be odd for you to sleep during the day, but I need to get some rest. Feel free to make yourself at home, read a book, or I can let you use my laptop."

Anthony's voice pulls me out of my own head once again. And his mention of rest suddenly makes me aware of my immense exhaustion. My sleep pattern is always thrown off due to these nighttime immortality attempts, and I realize I've been awake for nearly twenty-four hours.

"Um, I could actually sleep, if that's alright."

I meet his gaze, and his face softens. "Of course, Rose." He starts walking towards his bedroom. "You can take the bed. I can get you a shirt and some shorts to wear, if you'd like, though they'll be a little big on you."

His words hit me square in the chest. *You can take the bed.* There's only one bed. And my heart rate picks up again as I follow him into the room. Blackout curtains line the windows but hints of sunlight peek through the bottom of the fabric where it met the polished concrete floor.

"Where will you sleep?" I ask. "You don't have a couch."

"I can make do on the floor for one night." His back is to me as he digs in some drawers, pulling out a plain black t-shirt and a pair of plaid boxer shorts. Turning back to me, he asks, "Are these okay?"

I swallow before nodding and gingerly take the clothes from him. "Anthony, I don't want you to sleep on the floor because of me." I eye the large king-size bed centered in the room. "The bed is large enough. We could share."

Internally, I beg my body not to push blood to my cheeks. *You are a grown-ass woman, Rose Miller! Act like it!* Clearly, my brain hates me because I hear myself blurt out, "It's my favorite trope!" *Goddamn it!*

Anthony just stares at me, confusion written all over his face.

I cringe before rushing into an explanation. "You know, a romance trope? The main characters are on a long journey and stop at a seedy inn for the night. There's only one room and one bed they're forced to share. The forced proximity makes the sexual tension unbearable, pushing them to finally give in to their desire for one another."

It's like an out-of-body experience. I hear myself speaking, but I cannot stop. "Not that there's tension here! I didn't mean that. I mean, you are incredibly attractive, and if that hug on the roof was any indication, you're very toned under those clothes." *SHUT. THE. FUCK. UP. ROSE!* "Not that you have to be toned to be attractive. That's not what I'm saying."

Finally my mouth gets the message from my brain, and I trail off, completely mortified at the word vomit I just spewed.

Anthony's eyes have been widening more and more with each ridiculous word I utter, his strange pupils dilating. I clutch the borrowed clothes to my chest, turning to rush to the bathroom. "I'm just going to change!" I yell as I slam the door behind me. *Oh. My. GOD.*

***

I take much longer than needed in the bathroom, trying to talk myself into going back out there and acting normal. Finally, I open the door and slide out into the bedroom, which is now dimly lit by the lamp on the bedside table.

Anthony steps into the room seconds after, his hand automatically massaging the back of his neck as he peers at me warily. "Um, about the sleeping arrangements."

He trails off, and I jump in with, "Anthony, I'm sorry. I'm so tired, so please ignore my ramblings. If you're comfortable sharing the bed,

I'm comfortable with it. We can each stay on our own sides." I peer at him through my lashes as his hand relinquishes the grip on his nape and, instead, slides through his hair.

He puffs out a breath before saying, "That should be fine." He sees the clothes I'm holding and rushes to offer space on top of the dresser to set my things. I cross the room, setting my clothes down and turn back to face him.

He's standing in the same spot, his eyes wide once again as he stares at my legs. I see his Adam's apple bob in a swallow before his eyes finally trail up my body and meet my gaze. Clearing his throat, he motions to the side of the bed I'm standing closest to. "Uh, is there anything you need before we, um, retire?"

I stifle a giggle before answering, "No, I'm fine." I turn down the covers, slipping in and settling back on the pillows. I turn to watch him do the same before he turns off the lamp, plunging us into darkness.

Suddenly the silence roars in my ears, and it's like his atoms are tugging at my atoms under the blanket. I have the urge to slide over to him, to curl myself into him. And by the shifting of the blankets I can feel next to me, I gather he must feel the same pull. I force myself to lie still, counting my breaths to keep them even. We're two adults who barely know each other. We can handle this.

"Rose," his throaty whisper sends a bolt of lightning straight to my clit, and I stifle a gasp.

Not trusting my voice, I whisper back, "Yes, Anthony?"

I feel him turn to face me. "Why do you picture yourself alone with your books for eternity? Don't you want companionship?"

I release a sigh. "I wouldn't make a good companion for anyone, Anthony."

I hear a sharp intake of breath from his direction, and his answering words are almost angry. "Rose, that's absolutely not true."

I finally turn to face him, just making out his face as my eyes adjust to the dark. "I struggle with connection. I would disappoint anyone who tried."

"Oh, Rose." Slowly, he reaches his hand across the space between us, gently stroking my cheek, his fingers trailing down my jaw before he pulls back. "That's your childhood trauma talking. You know that, right?"

On some level, I do. But there's another part of me that has just succumbed to my brokenness. I close my eyes, knowing he won't accept any version of that as an answer. "Let's just get some sleep."

There's a long pause before he whispers, "Goodnight, Rose."

I roll over to face the other way before barely whispering, "Goodnight, Anthony."

***

It takes a long time for me to fall asleep, and yet it feels like just minutes later when my eyes shoot open again. My chest is heaving, sweat builds on my brow, and a low throb emanates from my body. The room is still. Light still spills out from the bottom of the curtains. The stillness from the other side of the bed lets me know that Anthony is asleep.

I lie there, staring at the dark ceiling, processing what woke me up. My breathing starts to even out, and I toss the covers off to allow myself to cool down a bit. Look, I've had the occasional sex dream, especially when it's been...well...a while since I was last with anyone other than my vibrator. But this dream was incredibly vivid and so hot.

And it starred the man currently fast asleep next to me.

That is when I get—in the words of Dr. Seuss—a wonderful, awful idea. I've noticed his small reactions to me, so he must reciprocate this attraction. And so what if, in the heat of the moment, he loses control and bites me? Isn't that how most vampire sex works? Surely, once he bites me, with his super control due to the coconut water, he'll realize what he's done and stop, right? No risk of him draining me, right? So, physically, I should be safe.

And what man—or vampire—wouldn't love to be awoken by sex with a woman he's attracted to? Yes, this is a perfect plan. Slowly and carefully, I slide across the bed to where Anthony sleeps, preparing to put this plan to action.

Chapter Eleven

DID YOU DO ANY RESEARCH?

Anthony

Rose's body is warm against mine, smothering me in a heat I'd gladly suffocate in. My hands find their way to her waist, sliding up her back before gliding back down to her ass. I give her a slight squeeze before pulling her lower body to mine, grinding the evidence of my arousal against her. Her lips trail wet kisses over my neck, her hands doing their own fair share of wandering. I feel her leg slide between mine, notching us together like puzzle pieces. Our hips move in tandem, building a delicious friction I haven't felt in a very long time.

This is, by far, the best dream I've ever had. The thoughts that plagued me as I fell asleep next to Rose must be the reason my subconscious dropped me here. Knowing she was close enough to reach out and grab, tug to me, kiss, and fondle, and pleasure—it was enough to make any man manifest this version of a dream. And I would take advantage of it for as long as the sandman allowed.

I press a kiss just below her earlobe, eliciting a small gasp from Rose, before trailing my tongue down the column of her neck. Finding the hem of her borrowed t-shirt, I slip my hands underneath, relishing the feel of her naked skin against my palms. I take my time caressing her back before sliding my hands to her ribcage, reaching my thumbs up to ghost over her already pert nipples. A moan slips from her lips, and I burrow my face in her neck, sucking her skin into my mouth, hoping to leave my mark on this dream Rose. My thumbs move back over her nipples, with a bit more pressure this time, and her back arches, pushing further into me.

Her hands slide from where they had been toying with my hair and one comes down to hold me through the thin boxer briefs I'm wearing. I hiss a breath through my teeth, and her grip tightens as her hand moves up and down my shaft. I pull my hands from under her shirt, grabbing the leg she had tucked between mine and shifting it so it rests atop my hip, opening her to me. I run my hand up her thigh until I reach the point that I can slide up the wide leg opening of the too-big boxer shorts she wears. I trail my fingers up her inner thigh to the crease of her hip before barely brushing her warm sex. *She isn't wearing any panties. This really is a dream.* Placing my finger at her clit, I press hard before sliding down to her opening and back up, trailing her wetness as I circle her clit and repeat the motions.

Her chest heaves as she whimpers my name, and a jolt of electricity seems to shoot through me hearing my name in her moment of plea-sure. The hand that had fallen loose over my clothed cock regains its grip before letting go and sliding in the front opening of my briefs. Her warm hand wraps around my dick, pumping twice before sliding up and over the head, massaging the bead of precum gathered at the tip. *This feels so real.*

Afraid to lose even a second of this dream woman, I slide my hand out of her shorts, dipping the finger coated in her arousal in my mouth. I groan. It's been too long since I've tasted a woman on my lips. I go to slide my hand back to her perfectly wet pussy when I hear the whir of a fan as my central air system kicks on. *That's odd. Why am I noticing that in a dream?* Rose notices my hesitation, pausing her movements as she leans away from me. "Anthony? Everything alright?"

Her question brings everything crashing down around me. This isn't a dream. This is real. And I came so close to ruining everything.

Quickly, I push her leg off my hip and untangle our arms before sliding out of the covers to stand next to the bed. I click on the bedside lamp, the soft light illuminating our precarious situation. My erection tents my boxer briefs and is not helped by the sight of Rose, pulling the covers back before moving to kneel on the bed before me. I slide my hands down my face, groaning at the unfairness of this situation. Why must I want this woman so badly?

Rose goes to grab my hand, but I dart out of her reach. "Rose, you can't touch me right now." My voice is stern but still coated in a layer of lust.

"Why?" she whispers.

"Because I need to get my arousal under control."

"I trust you, Anthony. I know you won't drain me."

My eyes shoot to hers, taken completely off guard with her statement. "Drain you? I'm not even going to bite you, Rose. That's not the issue here."

"Then what's the issue?" She looks so confused.

"Rose, that could have led to much more and would have ended catastrophically had I not come to my senses and realized it wasn't a dream."

Looking even more confused, she asks, "If you're not at risk of biting and draining me, how could it have ended badly?"

I just stare at her, waiting for her to tell me she's kidding. Did she think it would be this easy? But she just sits there, eying me expectantly. And then it hits me. *Could she really not know?*

A harsh laugh bursts through my lips, and her face falls. "Rose, did you do any research before you started this ridiculous endeavor to become immortal?" I start pacing around my bedroom. When she doesn't answer, I stop, staring pointedly at her. "Well?"

"I mean, not really. I just knew what I wanted." Her shoulders slump, and her gaze falls to her lap.

My frustration ebbs slightly at her defeated stance. My voice softens as I ask, "Rose, how do you think vampires are created?"

Without looking up, she says, "By biting?"

I can't keep the long sigh from escaping, and once again, my hands rake down my face. "Rose, vampires are not created through biting. They're created through penetrative sexual intercourse."

Her head jerks up, eyes meeting mine. "Wait, you're saying vampirism is a sexually transmitted disease?!"

Chapter Twelve

A PRETTY PENNY

Gavin

The shadows cast by the tall buildings surrounding me keep me hidden in a tight alley across the street from the building the couple entered. Last night, I saw the lights of the top-floor apartment turn on, and shortly after, the wind carried hints of their voices to me, letting me know they had gone to the roof. While I couldn't hear their conversation, the low cadence of his voice drifted down to me as if teasing me with knowledge I couldn't reach.

As the sun started to rise, their conversation had ceased, leading them back inside. I would benefit from sleep, but I couldn't risk leaving and losing her. If she left during the day, I'd never find her again. Which left me here, sitting in this dirty alleyway, waiting.

My mind spins, wondering what their relationship is. Humans are not permitted on this side of the city, but once in a great while you might see one. There's a market for humans, after all. I would know. *And she would bring me a pretty penny.*

Currently, my biggest concern is her remaining human. If he turns her, she no longer holds any value.

And if he doesn't turn her...

Well, I have to come up with a plan to extricate her from her companion without drawing his attention. I'm not sure how I am going to do that, but I don't have any other choice. *I must have her.* And luckily, I have plenty of time to brainstorm while I'm camped out here, waiting for her.

Chapter Thirteen

I DID NOT THINK THIS THROUGH...

Rose

"Wait, you're saying vampirism is a sexually transmitted disease?!" My head snaps up to look at Anthony, and his face is furious.

"Rose, why on Earth would you decide to completely alter your state of being, completely change your life *irreversibly*, without having done a sliver of research? Do you know how irresponsible that is? How dangerous?" His voice is rising in volume as he paces his bedroom floor. His hair is a complete mess from his hands constantly raking through it. *Or is that from my hands running through it just a few minutes ago?* I feel a blush creeping over my skin, remembering the position we were just in, how good it felt. And then it hits me how close I came to getting my wish. *Why did he have to stop?*

"Rose!" Anthony's shout jerks me back to the present, where he's stopped his pacing and is staring daggers at me.

"I'm sorry. I didn't know, okay? And should I have done a little more research on this? Yes, probably. But nothing you have told me through any of the time we've spent together has changed how I feel about this decision. So, I guess it doesn't really matter." I shrug, letting my eyes drop to my lap before peering back up at him through my lashes. I don't like seeing him this angry at me. Before he has a chance to further chastise me, I keep talking. "And I'm sorry I took advantage of the situation. I didn't realize that seducing you would directly lead to being changed. I mean, I'm not going to lie, I thought you might lose control and bite me, which would result in me getting my way anyway. Assuming, of course, that your super self-control from coconut water consumption held up. So, I guess I did mean to take advantage, but not in the way you think." My rambling comes to a close as I meet his gaze again and see his face is completely twisted in anger.

Anthony's chest heaves, and if it were possible, steam would be pouring out of his ears. When he speaks, he's no longer yelling. Instead, his voice is deadly quiet, which is even scarier. "Rose, are you seriously telling me that you were going to risk your life just to attempt this absurd dream you have? You were actually *hoping* I would lose control and bite you? Do you have no concern for your life?"

"I trust you, Anthony!" I barely get the words out before he's yelling again.

"You shouldn't! You shouldn't trust ANY vampire, Rose! Jesus Christ. I haven't drank directly from a human's body in over a century. I honestly have no idea how I would have reacted if I had actually bitten you! I very well could have drained you!" He collapses to sit on the end of the bed, his elbows landing on his knees, his face falling into his hands.

I want to reach out and comfort him, but I know my touch will not be welcome right now. "I'm sorry, Anthony. Really, I am."

"I would never have forgiven myself if I had done anything to hurt you, Rose." His voice comes out resigned, and I feel absolutely terrible for my lack of forethought. He's right. I have no business making decisions this big when I clearly don't think about the potential consequences.

Nothing I say right now is going to help the situation, so we sit in stilted silence for a long moment. Anthony finally lifts his head out of his hands and turns slightly to look at me. I offer him a sheepish smile and he just shakes his head. Anthony looks at the clock on his bedside table. "We still have a few hours. Let's try to get some decent sleep, yeah?"

I nod at him and shift myself back onto my side of the bed, sliding under the covers. He does the same before clicking off the lamp.

Before we fell asleep earlier, the silence was heavy with sexual tension, our bodies buzzing from the proximity to each other. Now, the silence is heavy with 'what ifs.' Anthony's touch lit me up like no other person has before. Feeling his hands on me, his mouth on me, hearing his lust-drunk voice utter filthy nothings in my ear—it was the best sexual experience of my life, and it didn't even make it to the actual sex part. What if I could have kept going? Even without knowing the STD part of it all, Anthony would have ruined me for anyone else. I just know it. But also, what if he *had* lost control with me? I would have ruined him in a completely different way.

I turn my head to face in his direction. "Anthony," I whisper. "I'm truly sorry. I would never want to put you in a position like that, and I'm sorry I didn't consider all possibilities. Please believe me."

The silence stretches for so long that I think he's already asleep, but then he whispers, "I know, Rose."

I stare in his direction, waiting for my eyes to adjust so I can see him. I smile and whisper again, "Hey, Anthony?"

I feel him shift beside me, turning to face me as well. "Yes, Rose?"

"So, STD, huh?"

I hear a hushed chuckle. "I've never heard it referred to so crassly. But, essentially, yes."

Eternally curious, I ask, "How does that work, exactly?"

"We aren't entirely sure. We know that it takes a biological male and a biological female. So, we've gathered that it's much like pregnancy in that it takes the male sperm and the female reproductive system. But we haven't pinpointed what about the female contributes to the process. A male vampire can turn a female human. And a female vampire can turn a male human. But males cannot turn males. And females cannot turn females. So, we know it's not just the sperm. It's possible the female ejaculate is the contributor, but we can't say for sure."

He pauses, so I ask, "What if she doesn't come?"

"What?"

I roll my eyes. "Are there an overabundance of male vampires?"

"Not particularly, though I haven't reviewed the most recent census to be sure. Why?"

Men. "Well, Anthony, most women don't orgasm during penetrative sex. So, if they don't come, will the vampire change still occur?"

He doesn't say anything for a long moment. "Huh. That's an interesting theory. I'll have to look into the data to see if this was taken into account. Surely, it was. Plenty of female vampires are included in these studies. They wouldn't have allowed such an oversight, even though clearly men would have."

I laugh before reaching across the bed and patting his arm. "It's okay, Anthony. Just be more attentive in the future."

He growls. "You didn't seem to be complaining."

"Well, you stopped it before we got that far. Guess we'll never know."

"You're killing me, Rose."

I laugh before turning my back to him. "Goodnight, Anthony."

"Goodnight, Rose."

***

I doze off and on but never manage to fall into a deep sleep. And eventually, my growling stomach stops allowing me to even doze. I slip out of bed, padding through the loft to the kitchen. Anthony only has coconut water in the fridge, because why would he have anything else? I grab a bottle of water, gulping down half the bottle. But it's not enough to assuage my hunger.

Quietly, I freshen up in the bathroom, using Anthony's toothpaste on my finger in my best attempt at brushing my teeth. I change my clothes, leaving his borrowed shirt and shorts folded neatly on the vanity. Anthony is still fast asleep when I leave the bathroom. Wandering back into the main room of his loft, I search out a pen and paper to leave him a note. I find a magnetic notepad on the fridge with a pen attached. I jot down a note and rip the paper off, leaving it on the kitchen counter for him to see.

As quietly as possible, I call the elevator and slide the door closed before heading downstairs. How hard can it be to find some human food?

***

The answer is *hard*. Super hard. I did not think this through. There are no human food establishments anywhere close by. A quick search on Google Maps shows no restaurants or grocery stores anywhere remotely close to me. And of course there aren't. No humans live on this side of town! What was I thinking? I wasn't. And that's my eternal problem, apparently. I don't *think* about anything.

I had wandered a few blocks from Anthony's apartment building, so I turn to start heading back, but I run headfirst into a tall body. Before I have a chance to fall, hands reach out and grab my elbows, steadying me before I land on my ass on the hard ground.

"Whoa, there. You alright?"

I look up to see who caught me. He's tall, wearing black Dickies cargo pants and a red flannel shirt. He has shoulder-length, brown hair, partially hidden under a black slouch beanie. He's wearing black Ray-Bans that have square frames and yellow-tinted lenses. The best way I can describe them is retro nerd. His full beard is neatly trimmed. The look is all pulled together with a pair of black leather lace-up boots that stop just above the ankle. A hipster vampire.

"Um, sorry about that. Thanks for catching me." I shake off the hold he has on my elbows, and he slides his hands in his front pockets.

"Are you lost? You're obviously not from around here," he states.

"Um, no, I was just on my way back to a friend's place. I was looking for food, but that was a lost cause." I start to edge around him, but he stops me.

"I know a place nearby. It's not on the maps. I could show you if you want?" His smile reaches his eyes, seeming genuine. And his body language doesn't suggest aggression. My stomach takes that moment to growl loudly, reminding me how hungry I really am.

Noticing my hesitation, he adds, "It's really close, and we could get you back on your way pretty quickly."

Deciding I have no better option, I nod. "Lead the way...?"

"Gavin."

"Gavin. I'm Rose."

"Lovely to meet you, Rose. Let's get you something to eat."

CHAPTER FOURTEEN

GODDAMN HER OBSESSIVE DREAM!

Anthony

I awake with my face buried in the pillow I have clutched to my chest. Before I open my eyes, I take a deep inhale, breathing in the rainy wildflower scent that comes with the adorably infuriating woman currently occupying my apartment. My thoughts drift back to last night, when I had her pulled tight against me, my hands free to roam over her supple body. I redirect my train of thought before I lose myself to arousal all over again. A small chuckle escapes me as I recall her calling vampirism a sexually transmitted disease. Her brain works in a way that is entirely mysterious to me.

But then I go back to the moment I realized she had been hoping I'd lose control, biting her in a craze of lust. Anger courses through me again at the reminder of her lack of basic self-preservation instincts. It shouldn't have surprised me, considering how we met. But the idea of her walking around in the world, willingly throwing herself in front of danger, submitting to the mercy of others, it terrifies me.

I open my eyes, expecting to see her still asleep on the other side of the bed, but it's empty. I sit up, straining to hear sounds of her, anything to give away her location or what she's doing. But the apartment is silent. Too silent.

Concern quickly replaces my anger, and I pull myself out of bed, noting as I do that the bathroom is empty. She was fine when we went to sleep earlier. Did she wake up and need some space from me? I leave the bedroom, hoping to find her curled up in one of my armchairs, but her absence is glaring.

She left.

Why would she leave?

And where would she go?

She can't get back into the donation center without me. And there's nothing else around here that would draw her attention. Again, terror grips me, thinking of her wandering around alone. Night will fall soon.

Glancing around the open loft, hoping for any sign of her that I missed, I see a note on the kitchen counter. My strides are long and quick, and I snatch the note up when I reach the counter.

You have no food here. You were woefully unprepared for human guests, mister. Going to find breakfast. Be back soon!

Goddamn it. Is she serious? I let go of the note, letting it float back down to the counter as I race back to my bedroom. I start pulling on clothes as I brush my teeth, shoving my feet in the closest shoes. I toss my toothbrush aside and race to grab my keys, determined to find her before any harm befalls her. It's my fault she's here, after all. God, why didn't I think of *food* for her? I should have known that she would be reckless enough to traipse around this area on her own. She probably didn't even stop to realize it *was* reckless. *Fuck!*

Once I get to the bottom floor of my building, I sprint out the front doors, looking in both directions, hoping I'll get lucky and her smiling face will be heading right toward me. No such luck. I take off in the direction of the donation center, assuming she'll go in a direction familiar to her.

After I go a few blocks without seeing any sign of her, I start to panic, my thoughts spiraling through the worst-case scenarios. I need to focus. If she was accosted by another vampire, the likelihood of there being signs of that encounter are high. She would have struggled, attempted to get free. Right? *Or would she have willingly gone with someone who offered false promises of immortality?* Goddamn her obsessive dream!

Most American vampires wouldn't have the sense of control or finesse to lure her to another location. Most, but not all.

One in particular pops in my mind.

And if he took her, it might already be too late.

Chapter Fifteen

I WILL FACE THE CONSEQUENCES OF MY OBTUSE NATURE

Rose

Gavin immediately begins leading me deeper into Vampire-Land—*seriously, someone should coin that!*—as the sun begins to set. The once empty streets start to fill with people—*vampires*—going about their normal lives. But Gavin maneuvers us down dark alleys and back streets, keeping us out of the main flow of traffic. At first, I think nothing of it since it's what Anthony did the night before. But as we keep walking, I grow more and more nervous. I don't know where I am anymore, and I'm not certain I could find my way back to Anthony's or to the blood donation center.

What was I thinking? God, I am an idiot. He's not leading me to food. I *AM* the food! I willingly let a strange man—VAMPIRE—lead me away from safety. They say to never let someone take you to a second location. Well, not only did I let someone lead me to a second location, I let a VAMPIRE do it. No wonder Anthony gets so frustrated with me. I truly have zero sense of self-preservation. And now my luck has run out, and I will face the consequences of my obtuse nature.

Seeming to sense my internal spiral, Gavin turns to me with a smile. "So, Rose, what brings you to our side of town?"

I'm not sure what I'm going to do about this mess I've gotten myself into, and it makes me hesitant to share much information with him. "Um, just visiting a friend."

His brow furrows. "It's odd to see a human with a vampire friend. That's sort of frowned upon."

"Uh, yeah..." I trail off, unsure how to respond to that statement. Sweat starts to bead on my forehead, and my heart is racing.

"We're almost there," he states as his hand finds my elbow, herding me towards a dark intersection.

I try to pull away, but his grip tightens, pulling me along as we turn the corner onto a deserted road. It appears we are on the backside of a commercial street, lined with windowless doors and dumpsters belonging to each business. My breath is coming in uneven pants, and I'm starting to feel like I can't pull in enough air.

Still holding my elbow, Gavin opens a nondescript door, showing a dark hallway inside. He ushers me in ahead of him, and I try to turn quickly to break our contact and scoot out the door. But he blocks my way out before the door slams shut, locking me in the darkness with a predator.

Chapter Sixteen

IT'S A WIN-WIN.

Gavin

Just as the door closes, Rose starts speaking. "Gavin, please. Please don't do this. I know I was easy prey, but there is someone who will be very worried about me, and I don't want him to blame himself for my stupidity. And that's exactly what he will do. Please, please just let me go back. Please don't hurt me." As she's pleading, she's backing further into the dark space. Even if she had the ability to see in the dark, she's not even attempting to assess her surroundings. She's just staring at me, wide-eyed fear plastered on her face. She's about to back into a table and potentially hurt herself, so I lurch forward to stop her from falling backwards.

Letting loose a blood-curdling scream, she turns to run and promptly flips herself over the same table I was hoping to shield her from. She hits the ground hard with a grunt. Quickly, I flip the lights on and rush around to help her up. Her knees are pulled into her chest, arms locked tightly around herself. She's buried her head, and her shoulders shake with sobs. I go to pat her shoulder to offer some sort of comfort, but she flinches, hurriedly scooting herself away from me.

"Please, please, please," she gasps out between sobs.

Her reaction to all of this is startling, and I realize I need to take a different approach. Slowly, I sit down in one of the wingback chairs near her. Raising my palms in a surrendering motion, I speak softly, "Rose, I am not going to hurt you. I'm going to feed you, just like I said."

She's still crying, but her body is no longer wracked with sobs, and she's breathing easier.

"I didn't mean to frighten you. If you'll stay here, I'll give you some space while I make you something to eat." Her eyes dart around the room, and her thoughts are clearly written on her face. "Rose, I know you're tempted to run from this place as soon as I walk away, but now that people are out and about, the risk of danger for you is much greater. I promise you are safe here. I have no intention of hurting you."

Confusion mars her features. "If you're not going to hurt me, why did you bring me here?"

I give her a small smile. "Why don't I make you some food, and then we can talk?"

She nods, and I stand, making my way behind the bar.

Before I begin preparing her food, I watch her ease out of her defensive position and finally take in the room. It's windowless, with a large gas fireplace being the focal point on the main wall. If someone asked me to describe this place, I would say decadent. It's all dark, rich colors, expertly curated to create an intimate atmosphere. The walls are painted a deep burgundy, perfectly pairing with the gray stone of the fireplace. Dark teal wingback chairs and black leather Chesterfield sofas fill the room, creating multiple seating areas. Antique end tables and coffee tables are perfectly placed throughout. The back wall contains the bar, lined with black leather barstools. Empty, vintage alcohol bottles line the shelves behind the bar, adding an authentic touch to the speakeasy I've dedicated my life to.

There's one door, directly across from the curve of the bar that leads into the front of the building, which masquerades as a tobacconist. *Masquerades* might not be the right word. I do actually source and sell high-end tobacco products, but people only buy them to be granted entrance to this lounge. While we vamps might not be able to get the same nicotine buzz we did when we were humans, many of us still enjoy the smell and ritual surrounding tobacco.

The hallway we entered from has a door to the all-gender bathroom and a door to the staircase that leads to the apartments above the business. Hopefully, she'll allow me the chance to show her more once she's finished eating.

Rose settles herself on one of the sofas, and I finally head to the small kitchen accessed behind the bar. Unsure of any potential dietary restrictions, I try to cover all my bases, quickly cooking some eggs and bacon, toasting a piece of rye bread, and scooping some fresh fruit salad into a small bowl. I place all this on a tray with a glass of water and head back to my guest.

Her eyes grow wide as I walk toward her with the tray of food. I set it on the table in front of her, and she quickly leans forward to snag a piece of bacon. I choose an armchair across from her, careful not to spook her again.

"Why do you have this food?" she asks in between bites.

"Well, I have a proposition for you." I do my best to keep my body language docile and inviting.

She stops chewing, worry crossing her face. With a swallow, she asks, "What kind of proposition?"

I mull over my words, finally deciding to ask a question of my own first. "Before I explain, I'd like to ask why you're on our side of town. Why are you really here, Rose?"

Her eyes fall, and she starts picking apart the piece of toast. "It's a long story."

"I'm sure it's not that long. Please, indulge me."

She hesitates for a moment but then finally blurts out, "I was hoping to be turned into a vampire."

I was not expecting that.

Well...that might not bode well for my intentions then...

"And why is that, Rose?"

Her eyes dart to mine. "Really? You really want to know? No lecture about how nothing could possibly be worth this stunted version of life? You're not going to reprimand me for not taking my safety more seriously?"

My eyebrows rise so high, I'm sure they're hidden under my beanie at this point. There's certainly a story here. "No lectures, no judgement. I just want to understand."

Her features soften, and her shoulders loosen. "I just want to live a long, quiet life where I get to soak up every romantasy book the world has to offer. I want to live hundreds, thousands of lovely adventures. I want to experience the grandest romances and the most devastating heartbreaks. But I want to do it all safely from the pages of books."

Interesting. My plan could still work.

Leaning forward, I ask, "What if you could do all of that without becoming immortal, Rose?"

Curiosity graces her face. "How?"

I gesture around us at my opulent lounge. "I run a speakeasy, where I offer freshly tapped human blood."

Said blood drains from her face, and her hands start to tremble.

"Wait, Rose. Let me explain. I promised you were in no danger, and I meant it."

She nods, but the fear is still present.

"This building is six stories high. The main floor fronts as a tobacconist, with this lounge hidden behind it. But the five floors above this have been renovated into ten apartment units. I live in one of them and five others are currently occupied by happy, healthy humans."

Her brows furrow in confusion, but I see her easing a little more, beginning to understand.

"It's rare that humans and vampires cross paths anymore, but when I do, I take the opportunity to make my offer. The humans that live here have all their expenses paid, all their needs met. They want for nothing. All I require in return is a regular supply of their blood. I never take more than the human body can afford to lose. The humans that have accepted my offer are all much like you, unhappy with their day-to-day, yearning for an easy, quiet life. And I give that to them. See, vampires miss the taste and feel of warm human blood. We're not meant to drink from cold, sterile blood bags. My system offers the luxury of fresh blood, without the violence. It's a win-win."

I lean back in my chair, crossing an ankle over my knee. I can see her gears turning, and I'm pleased to have intrigued her. She's considering it.

"I can build wall-to-wall bookshelves in your apartment, keep you stocked with any and every romantasy book your heart desires. You could find companionship with the other humans, to whatever extent you're comfortable. One of the humans here is a chef and happily took on the task of preparing meals for those who live here. I have the finest ingredients brought to me via my connections to the human side of town. You could live the rest of your days, happily disappearing into story after story."

I pause, admiring the gleam in her eye as she imagines what her life could be here.

"So, what do you say, Rose?"

Chapter Seventeen

I MEAN, WHY NOT?

Rose

"So, you just want me to be"—I make sure to exaggerate the air quotes on the next words—"on tap? Like, a fucking specialty beer?" *What in the vampire hell is going on here?*

Gavin just laughs. "I guess so, yeah. I want you to offer your blood to me so I can sell it to my patrons. You'd give up a bit once a week. I don't offer all...*flavors*...every day. And you would be provided a whole regimen of vitamins and minerals to avoid anemia."

"And there are other humans who live here and provide you with...product?"

Another laugh from Gavin. "You're funny. I like your wit, Rose. And yes, I can introduce you to a few of them. And I can give you a tour of the apartments. Whenever you're ready."

Whenever I'm ready.

Whenever I'm ready?

It's like he's taking for granted that his offer is too good to pass up. I stare at him, sitting smugly in his pompous armchair. *Can an armchair be pompous? If this armchair were sentient, it would definitely be pompous.*

Tired of sitting in my silence, Gavin says, "I'm sure you have questions. Ask away."

I narrow my eyes. "So, is this offer made to just any human you happen to find? Or is this an exclusive offer?" My sarcasm is my armor, and I hide behind it while I try to figure out what I'm going to do here. Can I leave? If I turn down his offer, will he let me?

Do I want to turn down his offer?

Gah, no, Rose! Do not get sucked in by this hipster vampire!

Unaware of my inner turmoil, Gavin answers my question. "I offer it to most humans I come across. Supply is limited, and I need to take whatever options I have. But your blood," he pauses, inhaling deeply. "Your blood smells like a rainy spring day. Vampires would pay top dollar to drink your blood just to experience the nostalgia of a cold beer on a hot day, dancing in the rain with their lover, basking in the smell of fresh-cut flowers." Another deep inhale. "The perfect blonde ale."

Gag me. What a fucking weirdo!

"You're coming off a little strong, my dude."

He chuckles. "My apologics."

I do have so many questions, but I don't even know where to start. And honestly, I keep thinking that Anthony would be so disappointed if I chose this path. Then again, do I want to go back to writing obituaries for a living? What Gavin is offering literally solves all my problems. Now that I'm thinking about it, I had no plan for after I was turned into a vampire. I guess I would still need to find a job, and I have no idea what I'm qualified to do on this side of town. I'd still be working my days away just to afford my living expenses. And that would never end.

But Gavin is offering an *all-expenses-paid* life package. And offering a steady stream of books to occupy my time. I would live a shorter life, but it would be a cush life. I mean, why not?

I don't read many billionaire romances, but when I do read one, I always want to scream at the FMC who still wants to work and demands financial independence. Nah, bro! I would happily let that hot as fuck billionaire pay my way through life. This isn't a hot as fuck billionaire, but it's a similar offer. I would be a fool to turn it down.

"I want to meet the other people who live here. I want to hear about this...offer...from them." I hold my head high, looking slightly down my nose at him. He needs to know that I'm in control here. And I might want to negotiate. What I'm negotiating, I don't yet know. But he needs to stay on his toes!

"Of course, we can head up there right now. I can even show you the unit you would live in." He stands and motions toward the hallway we came in from.

I stand and let him walk in front of me, leading the way to a door that I assume leads to the stairs.

But a loud pounding on the back door stops us as the person on the other side starts shouting. "Gavin! Gavin, open this door right now! I know you have her."

Anthony?

Chapter Eighteen

THAT DOUCHY, HIPSTER FUCK

Anthony

I pound on the exterior door relentlessly, not caring who sees or overhears. Gavin has her. I know he does. And I will not allow her to sell herself to him. To shackle herself to a vampire who would happily keep her locked away in order to sell her blood for the rest of her life. Everyone in the area knows about his speakeasy and how he stays in business. There's somewhat of a *gentleman's agreement* around here, keeping vampires from forcing their way to the humans upstairs. No one wants to disrupt the supply chain.

And when Rose dies, he will drain her of every last drop of her blood, ensuring she was worth the investment. Anger floods my body, flowing along with the adrenaline, and my fists start to leave small dents in the door.

"Gavin, open this fucking door right now!"

The door opens, knocking me back a couple steps. Gavin appears in the doorway, and my eyes rapidly scan the space behind him until I see her. All the breath empties from my lungs, and I double over, bracing my hands on my knees as undiluted relief fills me.

"What the hell is your problem, man?" Gavin is still standing there, and I have to resist the urge to throat punch him. I've never experienced a call to violence like this, but I think I could kill him right now. No, I *know* I could kill him right now. Pushing the urge down, I stand straight and shove past him to reach Rose. "Sure, come on in," Gavin mumbles behind me as he closes the door.

I grab Rose's face in my hands, tilting her head up to meet my eyes. Her hands automatically go to my forearms, sliding up to wrap around my wrists. "Are you okay? Did he hurt you?"

She smiles, and it's like new life being born in my old bones. "I'm fine, Anthony. He didn't hurt me. He made me breakfast."

My eyes narrow, and I turn to Gavin, without letting go of Rose. "Did you do anything to the food?"

He pushes his hands deep in the pockets of his black pants. His hazel eyes flash with anger as he answers, "No, I didn't do anything to her food. She was wandering around town right before sunset, looking for something to eat. I brought her here and fed her."

I turn back to Rose. "Why did you leave the apartment? You should have woken me so I could help you. I could have fed you and kept you safe." I try to keep my irritation at bay, not wanting her to think I'm angry with her. "I was so worried." I lean down, pressing my forehead to hers and taking a deep inhale of her floral scent. *When did I become this comfortable with touching her like this?*

"I'm sorry," she whispers. "I didn't want to wake you after the, uh, earlier *interruption* to your sleep. I thought I could deal with it on my own and come back before you were even awake. But after I got a few blocks away, I realized I had made a mistake." Her voice drops, only discernible due to our extremely close proximity. "You're right; I don't think things through."

I pull her to me, wrapping my arms around her back. She nuzzles her face into my chest and clasps her hands at my lower back.

Gavin decides now is a good time to interrupt our reunion. *Throat punching is still on the table.*

"Okay, well, Rose and I were just in the middle of something. Now that you know she's fine, you can see yourself out. Feel free to come back when the lounge is open." He gestures toward the door.

Rose must feel my anger building because she squeezes me tightly, burrowing herself deeper in my shirt. Reluctant to let her go, I turn my head to meet his stare. "I'm not leaving her here with you."

"That's not really your call, is it, my guy?" Gavin sneers at me.

Who the fuck does he think he is?

"'*My guy?* How old are you? You sound like a petulant child." My tone drips in condescension, letting him know exactly what I think of him.

That earlier flash of anger in his eyes reappears as a lingering flare. "Hey, there's no need to be rude. I'm just saying, Rose is a big girl. She can make her own decisions."

"Woman," I shoot back at him. "She's a woman, you misogynistic imbecile."

"Misogynistic? What are you—" But Rose cuts him off.

"That woman is right here and would appreciate it if you wouldn't speak about me like I'm not." She pulls away from me, and I catch the eye roll as she turns toward Gavin. "Can you give us a minute, please?"

He hesitates, knowing full well that I am going to try to talk her out of accepting whatever offer he's made her. Rose widens her eyes at him as if to say, *"Well?"* Finally, he huffs out, "Yeah, fine," before stomping off, leaving us alone in the dimly lit hallway.

I don't waste a single second. "Rose, whatever he's offering you, please don't take it."

She crosses her arms over her chest. "You don't want me to become immortal. But when someone offers me a chance to live out the rest of my human life reading books, that's not acceptable either. What do you want, Anthony?"

I reach for her arms, seemingly unable to go without some sort of physical contact between us. Gently, I unfold her arms and grasp her hands in mine, bringing them to my lips and pressing a kiss to her knuckles. "Rose, I want you to live. Really live. Not just be human. I want you to experience joy, love, excitement, pleasure. But I want you to experience it firsthand, not by reading someone else's adventures in a book. You deserve that, Rose. An immortal life surrounded by books would rob you of so much. But so would a human life, living locked in Gavin's building, surrounded by books. Books can't hold a candle to a life well lived."

She sighs, but I keep going. "I know you don't believe you're capable of these things, Rose, but you are. Just in the short time I've known you, you've made me feel more alive than I have in over a century. Don't let that douchy hipster fuck take your spark and hide it away. Don't let him rob the world of you and everything you bring to the table."

I press another kiss to her knuckles, and her eyes follow my lips. "You have a lot of faith in me for someone who has continuously acted annoyed by my presence since the moment you met me." Her eyes trail up to mine.

"I was never annoyed, Rose. You caught me off guard. You sparked warmth in my cold heart. And I didn't know what to do with that. I think we both have things we need to work on, and the stories we've written about ourselves could use some rewriting. Leave with me. Let me take you away from here so we can start rewriting. Please." I'm not above begging this woman. I will get on my hands and knees for her, if that's what it takes.

Her eyes dart to something behind me, and I can sense Gavin coming our way.

"Alright, that's enough time. Rose, shall we continue the tour?"

Her gaze slides back to mine, and I can only hope my eyes communicate my silent plea.

But her hands pull free from my grasp as she steps toward Gavin. And I feel like my heart is in a free fall. Have I lost her?

Chapter Nineteen

BURROWED INTO ME LIKE A TICK

Rose

The look in Anthony's eyes almost breaks me, and I realize he thinks I'm choosing Gavin. But I can't choose Gavin. Not when this man's—vampire's—disappointment cuts me deeper than any knife ever could.

As I step towards Gavin, Anthony's shoulders slump. And I rush to put him out of his misery. "Gavin, I can't accept your offer. But thank you for bringing me to a safe place and feeding me. I hope you'll respect my decision and let me leave." I steel my spine and hold my head up high, hoping I convey some sense of bravery.

Gavin looks taken aback. "You thought I wouldn't let you leave?" He shakes his head. "Rose, I'm not a monster. I wouldn't have imprisoned you here." He pulls a business card out of his pocket and hands it to me. "If you ever change your mind, let me know." He glances between me and Anthony before muttering, "Good luck."

I turn to face the brooding vampire who came here to save me. Defeat has fled his eyes and hope has filled them. He reaches for my hand. "Come on, Rose. Let's get you home."

Once we're outside, he reaches for my other hand, which still holds Gavin's business card. He quickly pulls it from my grasp, tossing it in a nearby dumpster. "Hey!" I feign outrage. "What if I want to leave my options open?"

He glares at me. "That should never be an option, Rose." He pulls me to him for another hug, and I feel him place a tender kiss on my crown. "You should always keep your options open, but giving up and spending the rest of your life in service to someone who only wants your blood? That's not an option. You deserve so much better, love."

My heart flutters at the term of endearment, and I relish this moment of being in his arms. It feels like the end of something, though I'm not sure what.

Finally, I pull away and ask, "What now?"

"Now, we sneak you over to the blood center and get you back to your side of town before they open for the day." He holds both of my hands, pressing kisses to my knuckles. "You'll need to stick close to me and try not to draw any attention."

I nod, and he lets go of one of my hands, twining his fingers in the other and leading me back through VampireLand.

***

The entire trek back to the blood center has been quiet. Even as Anthony leads us back to his lab, we don't speak. Unease hangs like a fog over us, neither of us willing to broach the subject of what comes next. What happens when I walk back through that fridge door?

Anthony drops my hand to unlock the door and ushers me inside, quickly closing the door behind us. He flips the lights on before turning back to face me, his hand automatically running through his hair.

I decide to be the one who breaks the silence. "So, should we exchange numbers?"

Anthony can't hide the grimace that crosses his features, his eyes darting to his shoes. My heart drops into my stomach, realizing he doesn't want to see me after this.

"Oh, I see," I whisper.

His gaze finds mine again before he says, "Rose, please don't take it personally. I want nothing more than to keep you in my life. But you need a clean break from me and my way of living. You need to break through your own glass ceilings and find passion in being human in your world. I don't want to risk being the thing that holds you back." He offers me a sad smile, a plea to forgive him for hurting my feelings.

"I get it." I take a big inhale and let it out in a long sigh. "Thank you, Anthony."

"No, thank you, Rose. It's been a pleasure to know you." He starts to reach for my hand but seems to think better of it and lets his arm drop back to his side.

I can feel the tears building behind my eyes and want to be away from him when the dam breaks, so I hustle to the walk-in fridge, wasting no time in opening the door. I step in but turn back for one last look. "Bye, Anthony."

He slides his hands into his jean pockets, and his shoulders shrug up near his ears. "Goodbye, Rose."

I turn on my heel, fleeing through the fridge, not stopping to think until I've made my way outside. The parking lot of the blood center is empty, my car being the only exception. Was it really only 24 hours ago that Anthony was sneaking me onto his side of town? I feel like I've lived an entire life since last being here. I make my way to my car, trying to hold it together. As soon as I hear the latch of the driver-side door closing, the tears break free. I bury my face in my hands and sob.

***

Life goes back to normal, but it's like there's a grey film over my eyes. Everything is muted. Food doesn't taste the same. Music doesn't bring me the same joy. Even the new romantasy series I'm reading just isn't hitting.

I spend the days writing obituaries and thinking about all the people on the other side of town who won't ever need obituaries. *People. Who am I kidding? Anthony.* My mind always leads me back to that cranky British scientist.

After allowing myself a few days to wallow, I decide to *try*. I try to do things that I know would make Anthony happy if he knew I was doing them. I attend trivia nights at my local bar and try to put myself out there. I've gotten to know some of the other regulars, and I enjoy myself when I'm there. But when I get home at the end of the night, I just wish I could tell him about it.

I found a place that offers goat yoga and tried that. After being peed on for the third time and laughing until I almost peed myself, I lose myself in the melancholy again because I want to see him roll his eyes as I describe the concept of doing yoga with baby goats.

Since I can write anywhere, I start spending one day a week at a local cat café. There's just something about the juxtaposition of writing about death while letting adorable kittens crawl all over my lap that really calms me. But again, my thoughts stray to Anthony and what he would say when I get home covered in cat hair.

I even started therapy. Working through my childhood trauma has been rough, but my therapist has helped me realize that Anthony was right. I am capable of loving and trusting other people. It won't come easy, but it'll be worth the effort. I wish I could tell him that. I wish I could thank him for believing that I'm capable of growth.

Despite all the progress, despite my attempts to actually live out in the world and not bury my head in a book, everything circles back to Anthony and how much I miss him. And I am starting to wonder if that will ever change. We didn't know each other long, or very well, but he burrowed into me like a tick—HA! *bloodsucker*—and I can't get him out. What is the point of all of this growth if I can't share it with the one person I've truly connected with?

I no longer want to live my life reading other people's stories. But I also no longer want to live this life if he's not in my story.

Chapter Twenty

PHANTOM WHIFFS OF RAIN DRENCHED WILDFLOWERS

Anthony

Weeks have passed since I last walked Rose through the blood center, sending her on her way back to a human life. And with every week, her absence doesn't fade. It's like her ghost haunts me, despite her being alive and well. When I lie awake in my bed, unable to stop thinking about her, I swear I can hear her breathing next to me. I can feel the heat of her body inches from mine under the sheets. I catch phantom whiffs of rain-drenched wildflowers.

For a while, each night I expect to open the walk-in door and see her standing there, ready with a snarky comment about how she doesn't give up that easily. But each night that she isn't there, I fall further into the idea that she actually listened to me. She actually chose to *live*. And imagining her living a full life fills me with a bittersweet ambivalence.

If I thought I had become disillusioned with my immortal life before I met Rose, I can definitively say that I've become even more weary with it since she walked away. I hold tight to the memories of her, replaying them over and over, grasping for the stirrings of life I experienced in her presence. But my memories are so few, so—desperate for a small piece of her—I bought a popular romantasy series and began reading it, hoping to experience the joy she gets from these books. I try to imagine her internal commentary as she reads, but all it does is remind me that she isn't here to tell me about it herself.

The days come and go, each one passing exactly the same as the last, and I have no idea how to get off this ride. So, I just keep trudging along, hoping that time will ease my ache for her. Rainy days are the hardest, when the petrichor hangs in the air, taunting me with half of her scent. Today, my walk to work was through a deluge, and I leave my dripping wet umbrella outside my lab door. Going through the motions, I turn on all the lights and get my equipment ready before heading to the walk-in to grab the day's samples.

When I open the door, her floral scent hits me like a smack in the face, and I close my eyes. I let my chin hit my chest as I inhale deeply, savoring the moment, knowing it won't last long.

"Anthony?"

Her small voice washes over me, and I nearly give myself whiplash as I throw my eyes open and shoot my head up to see her standing there.

Rose.

She's here.

And she's holding suitcases...

Chapter Twenty-One

INCREDIBLY MISGUIDED ATTEMPT AT ROMANCE

Rose

Seeing him again after all of these long weeks is like waking up after the best night's sleep. I just want to rush into his arms, but I don't want to push him too far right away.

"Rose?" His voice comes out strangled, and he clears his throat before continuing, "You're here." He steps toward me, hesitantly at first, but then he's suddenly inches away and is pulling me into his chest. Before I can stop myself, I bury my face in his chest, grasping at the back of his lab coat as if to pull him even closer to me. I can hear him murmuring my name as he presses kisses to my head, and I truly couldn't have imagined this going any better.

Finally, he pulls away, just enough to see my face, allowing me to keep my hold around his waist. "To what do I owe the pleasure, love?" His eyes twinkle with the flirtatious nature inflected in his words, and the corners of his mouth twitch up into a smile.

"Are you really happy that I'm here? Because I expected you to be furious." I know my eyes are pleading with him to take me in, to leave his anger behind. I can tell he sees it when his eyes soften, and he brushes a wild lock of hair behind my ear.

"Rose, I cannot begin to describe how much I've missed you. Of course I'm happy you're here." His eyes roam my face, lingering on my lips, before he leans down and presses the lightest of kisses to my mouth. Another brush of his lips across mine has me pressing up on my toes, following the kiss, and this finally shatters his control. His fingers tangle in my hair as his thumbs bracket my cheekbones. His tongue dances over the seam of my lips, and I open for him without a second thought. He wastes no time deepening the kiss, and I melt further into him with each caress of his tongue.

After a long moment, we break the kiss, each of us panting as we pull apart. He glances at the bags at my feet and shoots me a questioning look. "Care to fill me in, love?"

Nerves suddenly hit me as the moment of truth arrives. I made no backup plan here. I have no idea what I'll do if he turns me away. He sees my sudden change and gently strokes my cheek. "It's okay, Rose. Just tell me."

"Well, I, uh, I'm moving in." I steel my spine, hoping he sees I am not in the mood to negotiate this.

He looks startled, but he doesn't let go of me. "You're moving in?"

That's when the word vomit starts.

"Anthony, did you know your name means flower?" He opens his mouth to say something, but I don't give him time as I ramble on. "Yeah, it's of Greek origin and comes from the word 'anthos,' which means flower. At least, that's what Google tells me. And yes, I googled your name, okay? I was missing you and looking for some sign that this insane idea I had was the right thing. And to me, your name meaning 'flower', and my name being Rose was the best sign I could have gotten. Have you seen The Notebook? Who am I talking to? Of course you haven't seen The Notebook. Well, Ryan Gosling has this stupidly romantic line where he tells Rachel McAdams, 'If you're a bird, I'm a bird.'" I finally pause to take a breath. "Anthony...if you're a flower, I'm a flower."

Silence ripples around me as Anthony just stares at me, dumbfounded.

If you're a flower, I'm a flower? What kind of idiotic bullshit is that?! Why did I say that?! Oh my sweet baby Jesus, what the fuck is *wrong* with me? He's going to think I'm a fucking lunatic, and honestly, he wouldn't be wrong.

Seconds pass as I spiral into my own black hole of embarrassment, but then he starts laughing.

Laughing!

He's laughing at my declaration of love!

"I'm sorry, are you *laughing* at my incredibly misguided attempt at romance? That is rude, Anthony. Super fucking rude." I let go of him and cross my arms over my chest.

He manages to contain his offensive laughter and says, "Rose, I'm not laughing at you. I would never laugh at you. But...you must admit that line doesn't quite work the same when referring to plants. Though I deeply appreciate the sentiment." He winks at me, and it's like I'm seeing a completely different side of my broody, scientist vampire.

"Are you teasing me?"

"I'm sorry..." He has the decency to look chagrined.

"My point is, I want to be where you are, Anthony. I tried the whole 'living' thing like you suggested, and it was great and all, but I just wanted to tell you about my experiences. I wanted to share them with you. So, I decided—without your input because you refused to give me your phone number, so this is really your own fault—that

I am moving in with you. I sold my car, terminated my lease on my apartment, got rid of all my furniture, and managed to pack the rest of my life in these suitcases. I even got rid of all my books. Not before I got ebook versions of them, but still. I couldn't lug them through the blood donation center."

"How *did* you get in here with those? You must have had a terrible time sneaking around."

"Oh, no," I chortle. "I had to pay Blair a hefty chunk of change to let me sneak in here. There was no way I could do it without someone on the inside. She was happy to oblige."

"Ah, I see. Very fair." He slides his hands in his pockets and rocks back and forth on his heels as he smiles down at me.

"Seriously? That's the part you question? Not the part about me unilaterally deciding to move in with you? Not the part where I got rid of all my stuff and moved out of my apartment with nowhere to go? Seriously, Anthony, I have no backup plan. You should be livid right now." I start speaking in a mock British accent. "Rose, you have no sense of self-preservation and really should practice more fore-thought."

Before I can say anything else, he pulls me back in for another mind-melting kiss. Then he grabs my bags and leads me into his lab.

"Rose, you don't need a backup plan. I regretted letting you go the moment you left, and I've been aching for you every moment since. If you'll have me, I will give you the immortal life you were searching for. And I hope you'll live out your long years with me."

I'm afraid to speak. Afraid to burst the happy bubble growing inside my chest.

"Is that still something you want, Rose?"

I launch myself into his arms again, and he laughs as he stumbles.

"I don't think you realize what you're in for, Anthony," I tease.

His eyes turn very serious, and he grabs my face, keeping eye contact. "I do, Rose. I really do."

Chapter Twenty-Two

FUCKING FINALLY

Anthony

I waste no time texting my replacement to come to the lab. While I wait for a response from him, I tuck a few pouches of tested blood into my lab coat—not technically legal, but we're not suffering a shortage, so it shouldn't be missed. Once I get a text stating he's on his way, I scoop up Rose's bags, hand her the umbrella, and rush her out of the blood center as fast as I can. I got this woman back. I got her back when I never thought I'd see her again. It seems too good to be true. But she's really here.

My clothes are soaked through by the time we rush through the ground floor of my building. Once we're enclosed in the elevator, everything seems to slow down. The silence is heavy, weighed down by the immense, delicious tension surrounding us. And when we stop at my floor, I fling the door open, toss her bags to the side, and grab her into my arms. Instinctively, she wraps her legs around my waist, pulling my mouth to hers in a bruising kiss, and I head to the closest surface—my dining table.

Kicking chairs to the side, I sit her on the edge of the table, staying firmly between her thighs. I break our kiss, resting my forehead against hers. "Are you sure about this?"

Her eyes meet mine, searing into me with the emotion filling them. "I've never been more sure."

With those words, we desperately rip at each other's clothes, flinging articles across the room as we remove each one. When we realize we've both gotten each other down to our underwear, we pause a moment to appreciate what we're seeing.

My eyes trace her porcelain skin, starting at the divots in her collarbones, trailing down the slight cleavage spilling out of her black bra, down her soft belly to the black panties covering the delicious cunt I've been dying to taste again. I lick my lips, and she must read me like a book because she says, "Not yet, Anthony. Don't make me wait for this, please."

I meet her eyes, and the yearning in them could bring me to my knees. She needs our connection. She needs to solidify our future together. Who am I to keep her waiting?

Quickly, I unhook her bra, telling myself I will have a lifetime to worship her perfect breasts, her pert nipples, which are begging for my mouth.

Focus.

Tossing her bra aside, I glide my fingers under the hem of her panties, and she lifts her hips, allowing me to slide them over her ass and down her legs. Standing straight again, I bring my fingers to her opening, letting one dip inside to see how wet she is. I groan as I feel her slippery warmth, pulling my finger out and dragging her wetness to her clit. I alternate between circling and direct pressure, and she wraps her arms around my neck as her hips start to rock, chasing the orgasm.

"Anthony, please," she whines.

"Give me one, love. Just one so you're nice and ready."

I increase the pressure, speeding up my circles before she finally throws her head back with a cry, her body spasming as the orgasm washes over her.

Before the wave has fully passed, I notch the head of my cock in her entrance before thrusting in. Rose cries out again as her body stretches to accommodate me. After a few shallow thrusts, testing the water of what her body can handle, I give one hard push of my hips until I'm completely sheathed in her warmth, and I press a kiss against her forehead. "Fucking finally. No turning back now, love."

"Why would I want to?" she whispers, her breath heating my skin.

And I begin to move in earnest, grinding against her, hitting every angle inside of her until I find the one that brings out the most beautiful moan. My pace picks up, our pleasure intensifying until we've lost all rhythm. Her nails drag down my back as she claws for purchase. I grip her ass hard, knowing my fingers will leave bruises as I rut into her. We come together to a symphony of moans and cries. Her name leaves my lips in a prayer before I kiss her softly.

Not knowing how much time I have, I pull out of her, not caring about the mess we've made. I lift her in my arms, bridal style, and carry her to our bed. Once I get her settled, I go in search of the blood bags I pocketed before rushing back to her side.

Her eyelids are heavy, but her smile is soft. Sexy and lazy.

"How are you feeling, love?" I brush her hair away from her face.

Her voice comes out in a whisper. "Strange. But okay."

"You'll pass into unconsciousness soon, and when you wake up, it'll be done. You'll be thirsty, but that's what these are for." I hold up the blood bags before setting them on the bedside table, making a mental note to grab a cup from the kitchen so she doesn't have to drink straight from the bags when she wakes up.

"You'll be here when I wake up?"

"I won't leave your side, Rose."

With that, her eyes flutter closed, and I watch the subtle signs indicating that her body is changing.

***

Rose wakes up gradually, wincing when she finally sits up in bed. She fingers the hem of my t-shirt where it rests across her upper thighs. "Thank you for this."

I smile at her. "I thought you might be more comfortable if you didn't wake up completely naked. How do you feel?"

She takes a moment, as if taking stock of her body. "Sore. My eyes hurt. Oh! My eyes! I want to see them!" She moves as if to get out of bed but then stops when she realizes her energy has been drained. Instead, she falls back into the pillows.

I chuckle softly. "Easy there, your body just went through a lot." I hand her a thermos with a plastic straw, motioning for her to drink. She pulls the liquid into her mouth, closing her eyes when the taste hits her tongue. "Drink the whole thing, but drink it slowly."

I reach to the bedside table where my phone is plugged in. Opening the forward-facing camera, I turn it to her so she can see her eyes. The straw pops out of her mouth, leaving a drop of blood on the center of her lips. Her tongue absently darts out to clear it as she leans forward to examine herself in the camera.

"Wow..." Her fingers lightly trail over the permanent bruising under her eyes, but she's transfixed by the dark, hazel globes staring back at her. Her once brown eyes have been replaced with a beautiful kaleidoscope of color. Browns, greens, ambers. Like a pond. And it occurs to me that I get to spend the rest of my life gazing into these deep pools of color.

"You're beautiful, Rose."

Her gaze shifts from the camera to me, and she smiles. "You're stuck with me now."

I kiss her deeply before responding, "You brought me back to life, Rose. I'm not stuck with you. I'm eternally grateful that you chose to spend your life with me. And I am sorry for ever making you feel like your choices aren't valid. I should have never tried to make that decision for you, like I somehow know better than you because I've been alive so much longer. Hopefully, you can forgive my arrogance. I will spend the rest of our lives ensuring you never end up regretting this choice."

She kisses me back before whispering, "I could never regret this, Anthony. I love you."

"I love you, Rose."

I redirect her attention to the thermos, still half full of blood. "Finish drinking that, and you'll feel a little closer to normal."

She sucks on the straw again. Then, "No coconut water?"

I shake my head. "You need human blood after the change, but you'll be able to start living off coconut water immediately. And we need to get your paperwork squared away."

Rose reaches out and wraps her hand around the back of my neck. "Anthony, let's just take a moment to enjoy being together. Is that okay?"

I sigh as I lean into her touch. She shifts on the bed, and I slide into the space she made for me. Wrapping my arms around her, I tug her into my lap, relishing the feel of her against me.

"Of course, love," I whisper against her shoulder.

She quietly drinks the rest of her blood until the straw is making those annoying slurping sounds as she reaches the bottom. Smacking her lips, she sets aside the empty thermos before turning in my arms. "Okay, after today, I feel like you have no choice but to watch The Notebook. Let me reclaim some dignity by showing you what kind of romance I was going for."

A smirk plays across her face as I toss my head back in laughter.

"As you wish, Rose."

"'As you wish?' Are you trying to tell me you're a Princess Bride fan? We can watch that one next!" She bounds out of bed, presumably to get her laptop. As I watch her flounce around my apartment, wearing nothing but my t-shirt, I think back to Anne, and suddenly, all the anger I harbored for her is gone. Had she not taken my life, against my will, I never would have lived long enough to meet this incredible, chaotic woman. And what a sad life that would have been.

EPILOGUE

IT'S MY FAVORITE TROPE

Rose

One Year Later

I wring the water out of my hair into my towel before combing it and letting it lay damp and loose against my shoulders. I dab on some lip balm and smooth lotion over my skin. After throwing on one of Anthony's t-shirts—and nothing else—I give myself one more once-over in the mirror, lingering on my strange hazel eyes. I don't think I'll ever get used to those. Or the bruising under my eyes that gives me a little bit of that grungy, heroin chic look that was all the rage in the nineties. I get it without working for it! Too bad I'm a few decades late to the party.

Exiting the bathroom, I see Anthony sitting exactly where I left him when I got up to shower—one leg crossed over the other, back straight in his armchair, book in hand. My feet are silent on the bare floor, but I know he hears me coming. Still, he doesn't acknowledge me until I'm sliding into his lap. Smiling, he places his bookmark and closes the book, setting it on the table in between the two chairs.

"What part are you on?"

Wrapping his arms around me, he answers, "Well, they just got to the seedy inn. They're both exhausted and filthy from their journey.

Tempers are high. And the innkeeper lets them know there's only one room. They take it, of course. But when they get upstairs to their room, they quickly realize—"

I cut him off, "There's only one bed. Classic." I smirk at him.

His eyes turn mischievous before he says, "Well, it's my favorite trope."

I squeal as he gracefully lifts me in his arms, his book long forgotten, and carries me to our bed.

I run my tongue up the side of his neck to his ear, where I whisper, "But I just took a shower."

He tosses me on the bed, causing my shirt to ride up my thighs and over my hips, flashing the fact that I'm not wearing anything underneath.

"Really? Because from here, you look filthy."

I laugh as he crawls up the bed, kissing every inch of my exposed skin until he hovers over me. We share a sensual kiss before devolving into touching, gasping, moaning, pleasure. And after, as we whisper and giggle, all our limbs twined together, I send a silent thank you to romantasy authors everywhere. Without whom, I would not have developed an inflated sense of skill or illusions of grandeur that led me on a hairbrained journey to this man. And now, I get to spend eternity in his arms. Who needs self-preservation and forethought when you have a half-baked plan and stubborn pride?

Not me.

The End.

THANK YOU!

Kalie, this book would not have happened without you. Without the hour-long brainstorming call while you were driving. Without the many, many text messages from me asking vampire-specific questions, needing your scientist mind to think about what I don't. Without your introduction to Christopher Moore when we were in college. Without my sense of humor that has, without a doubt, been shaped by you. Without your sense of humor that adds layers I wouldn't have found. We're going on 25 years together. Here's to 25 more, overflowing with laughter and inside jokes. 25 more years of teaming up against our spouses, however unfairly, so we dominate any pop culture game. 25 more years with my soulmate.

Dana, thank you for being the female narrator for all of my books. Thank you for all the hard work you put into your craft. Your care and dedication shows through in each character you bring to life. I'm so grateful that you are who brought mine to life. Thank you for answering all my questions each step of the way.

Chad, thank you for all the hours you have to listen to me talk about books. I am trying to better fake enthusiasm when you do the same to me with your shows. But you know my facial expressions are too loud, and I have no control over them. Just know...I'm trying. And I love you. Thank you for being supportive of this insane thing I decided to do. It was not my brightest moment.

Mom, you're always my biggest cheerleader, even when I'm begging you not to be. It's clear that one of your strongest tenets as a parent is infusing your kids with the confidence you have in them. You see me and Mitchell in the way only a present, loving, supportive mother can. And I know you want us to believe in ourselves as much as you do. You want us to see ourselves as the amazing people you see. So, when I'm visibly uncomfortable with your praise, don't take it personally. I love you so much, and I appreciate you more than you know.

Dad, thank you for jumping on whatever bandwagon Mitchell and I have hitched our horse to. No matter what we've decided to do in life, you've been supportive and proud. I don't know many other dads who would not only shout praise from the rooftops for their daughter writing a ghost porn story, but would also gladly read that ghost porn story. Your openness and your support do not go unseen. I love you.

Caitlyn, thank you for everything. For knowing me so well that you can read right through me, even in text messages. ("Yes, I just babe'd you.") Thank you for always being there and for loving me exactly the way I am. Thank you for being my champion, my person. My best friend.

Caitlin and Nic, thank you for beta reading, once again. Your feedback is invaluable. You make me better.

To the content creators, BookTokers, Bookstagrammers that I've worked with over the past year, thank you. Vonnie, I'm looking at you! Thank you for taking a chance on an unknown, baby indie author. Thank you for reading and sharing my work. Being an indie author is hard, but you make it just a bit easier.

Lola's Legion, you guys are the BEST! Truly. Your support continues to blow my mind. Thank you for taking a chance on me and hanging out with me throughout this ride. Indie authors could not succeed without the team of people who help spread the word. Thank you for being mine.

To my readers, you're the reason we're all here. Thank you for picking up my book, for reading my story, for (hopefully) loving my characters. You've given me an incredible gift.

Here's to the end of my indie author journey...for now, anyway.

ABOUT THE AUTHOR

Lola B. Marie was born and raised in the Midwest. She's an avid Chiefs fan, a terribly competitive fantasy football player, and a romance reader. She lives with her husband, son, dogs and cat. All the pets are boys and she doesn't mind being outnumbered. When she isn't writing or with her family, you can find her hanging at Bedpost Books, her favorite locally-owned bookstore in the Midwest. She's also usually listening to one of a hundred podcasts while drinking Dr. Pepper and eating some sort of gummy candy.

As a typical pissy Pisces, she's also a dreamer who never expected one of her dreams to come true. Writing was always something she enjoyed but she never thought she'd write something to completion. And now she's a published author. Live your dreams, kids. They're possible if you want them to be.

9 798999 863126